The Elijah Project

The Enemy Closes In

Other Bill Myers Books You Will Enjoy

The Elijah Project
On The Run
The Enemy Closes In
Trapped by Shadows
The Chamber of Lies

The Forbidden Doors Series
The Dark Power Collection
The Invisible Terror Collection
The Deadly Loyalty Collection
The Ancient Forces Collection

Teen Nonfiction
The Dark Side of the Supernatural

The Elijah Project

The Enemy Closes In

Bill Myers

with James Riordan   *bestselling author*

ZONDER**kidz**

ZONDERVAN.com/
AUTHOR**TRACKER**
follow your favorite authors

For Drew Sams:
A man of compassion with a heart for youth.

Zonderkidz

The Enemy Closes In
Copyright © 2009 by Bill Myers

Requests for information should be addressed to:
Zonderkidz, *Grand Rapids, Michigan 49530*

Library of Congress Cataloging-in-Publication Data

Myers, Bill, 1953-
    The enemy closes in / Bill Myers with James Riordan.
      p. cm. — (Elijah project ; bk. 2)
    Summary: Zach and Piper, with divine assistance, continue to seek their kidnapped
parents and protect their little brother, Elijah, from the evil Shadow Man, who places
temptation in their path in the form of a beautiful runaway.
    ISBN 978-0-310-71194-0 (softcover)
    [1. Supernatural — Fiction. 2. Christian life — Fiction 3. Runaways — Fiction. 4.
Healing — Fiction. 5. Adventure and adventurers — Fiction. 6. Brothers and sisters — Fiction. 7.
Angels — Fiction. 8. California — Fiction.]
I. Riordan, James, 1936 — II. Title.
PZ7.M98234Ene 2008
[Fic] — dc22

                                  2008001426

Published in association with the literary agency of Alive Communications, Inc., 7680 Goddard Street #200, Colorado Springs CO 80920, www.alivecommunications.com.

Zonderkidz is a trademark of Zondervan.

Editor: Kathleen Kerr
Art direction: Merit Alderink
Cover illustration: Cliff Neilsen
Interior design: Carlos Eluterio Estrada

Printed in the United States of America

09 10 11 12 13 14 15 • 22 21 20 19 18 17 16 15 14 13 12 11 10 9 8 7 6 5 4 3 2

Table of Contents

For our struggle is not against flesh and blood, but against the rulers,
against the authorities, against the powers of this dark world and against
the spiritual forces of evil in the heavenly realms.

—Ephesians 6:12

Chapter One

The Chase Continues

The tires of the old RV squealed around the turn.

Piper flew across the motor home, slamming hard into the door. "Zach, slow down!"

Of course her big brother didn't listen. What else was new? But this time he had an excuse. Driving the RV up the winding mountain road was tricky. Especially when people were chasing them.

Especially when those people wanted to kidnap their little brother.

Especially when they had guns.

He took another corner, throwing Piper the opposite direction. "Zach!"

He grinned, pushing aside his handsome black hair—handsome if you like haircuts that look like they were trimmed by a lawn mower.

Throwing a look out the back window, Piper saw the green van closing in.

She glanced at six-year-old Elijah. He was sound asleep. Although she loved him dearly, the kid was definitely odd. He seldom, if ever talked, but he always seemed to know things no one else did.

Then there were the miracles—healing a girl in the hospital, raising a puppy from the dead. Of course they tried to keep the stuff secret, but people always found out.

Which was probably why the bad guys were after them.

Which was probably why their parents had been kidnapped and hidden in these mountains. Someone very evil was using them as bait. And Piper and Zach were the only ones who could save them.

"What if it's a trap?" Piper had asked as they started out on the journey. "What if Mom and Dad didn't send that message wanting us to rescue them?"

"Then it's a trap," Zach shrugged. "What other choice do we have?"

Of course he was right. It was just hard to remember little details like that when you were being thrown around a motor home like a human ping-pong ball.

They took another corner, faster and sharper than all the others.

"ZACH!"

●

The driver of the green van was a skinny guy by the name of Silas. He was shouting to his red-haired passenger, Monica. "Are you sure they're going to break down?"

"That's what Shadow Man said."

"Right, but—"

"Has he ever been wrong, before?" she asked.

"No, but—"

"Then shut up and keep driving!" (Monica was not exactly the polite type).

A third voice called from the back. "Shadow Man—he's like my hero."

Silas and Monica rolled their eyes. They always rolled their eyes when Bruno spoke. He was a huge man with a tiny brain.

"Wanna know why?" he asked.

"Why?" Silas said.

"'Cause he brought me and Monica together."

Monica stole a look over her shoulder. As always, the man was all misty-eyed and ga-ga over her.

As always, she felt her stomach churn.

And, as always, she answered in her most pleasant screech. "Put a sock in it!"

"Yes, my sweets." He sighed dreamily. "Whatever you say."

●

The RV gave a loud *clunk.*

"Oh, no!" Piper cried "What's that?"

"I don't know." Zach pressed on the gas, but it did no good. *CLUNK! CLUNK!* They were definitely slowing.

"There's a gas station," Piper pointed to the right. "Pull in there."

"And just wait for those creeps to grab Eli?" Zach argued.

CLUNK! CLUNK! CLUNK!

Piper glanced to her little brother, who was now wide awake and looking out the side window. Not only looking, but grinning and waving.

Piper followed his gaze to the road. No one was there.

CLUNK! CLUNK! CLUNK! CLUNK! The engine finally stopped.

Zach dropped the RV into neutral and coasted the rest of the way into the station.

●

"LOOK OUT!" Monica screamed.

Silas looked up just in time to see an old hitchhiker standing in the middle of the road. He hit the brakes. They skidded out of control and swerved, barely missing the old man.

"WATCH IT!"

Now they slid toward the guardrail and a 200-foot drop-off.

Silas cranked the wheel hard, and the tires smoked ... until they hit the rail and bounced back onto the road.

"WHAT WERE YOU DOING?!" Monica demanded.

"I'm trying to keep us alive!"

"You almost got us killed!"

"I'm not the one standing in the middle of the road!"

"The old coot!" Monica looked back over her shoulder. "He could have gotten us all—" She stopped. "Wait a minute, where did he go?"

Silas glanced into the mirror. Try as he might, he could not see the old man.

"Did we, uh, squash him?" Bruno asked.

"I don't think so." Silas started to slow.

"What are you doing now?" Monica said.

"We better go back and check."

"We're not checking anything!"

"But—"

"If he wants to get hit, that's his business. We got some brats to catch!" Monica turned back to the RV in front of them. There was only one problem.

"Where is it?" she asked.

Silas searched the road before them and saw the same thing.

Nothing.

The motor home they'd been chasing all this time was nowhere to be seen. "Where'd it go?" Bruno asked.

"I don't know." Silas frowned. "They were right in front of us a second ago."

"Well step on it!" Monica shouted. "Don't let them get away!"

●

"Did you see that?" Zach asked. He watched as the green van continued up the highway, passing them and the gas station.

"They didn't even see us!" Piper said. "They were too busy swerving and skidding."

Zach searched the road. "I wonder why."

"Maybe they were trying to miss a deer or something."

Zach shook his head. "No, there was nothing there." He glanced into the mirror to see Elijah sitting in his seat smiling back at him.

Piper spotted him too. "Looks like the little guy knows something we don't."

Zach nodded and let out a weary sigh. "So what else is new?"

●

Mom and Dad sat chained to opposite walls in the cold, dark room.

"How are you holding up?" Dad asked. His voice was hoarse and cracked from lack of water.

"I just can't stop thinking about the kids," Mom said.

He heard the worry in her voice and nodded. "We just have to ..." He swallowed back the emotion in his voice and tried again. "We just have to be strong."

Outside, there was the rattling of keys. The door creaked open, and a guard just slightly smaller than a semitruck entered the room. "Time to see the boss," he grunted as he stooped to unlock their chains.

"Please ..." Mom's voice quivered. "Not again. There's nothing we can tell him."

"It'll be all right," Dad said. But inside he didn't believe it for a second.

"I just can't face him." Mom began to cry. "The way he burrows into my thoughts with those awful eyes."

"Stop your whining." The guard hoisted each of them to their feet. "It'll be over soon enough." He pushed them into the dimly lit hall. "If you're lucky."

Chapter Two

The Plan

"I just feel like we deserted them," Cody said as they entered the cluttered garage.

"Them?" Willard, his pudgy friend with curly hair said. "Or *her?*"

"Her, who?" Cody asked.

"Her, *Piper*," Willard answered.

"What are you talking about?" They walked around another one of Willard's failed inventions, *The Nuclear Powered Dental Flosser*—a giant, two-story machine designed to automatically floss your teeth while you slept. Not a bad idea, except instead of cleaning your teeth, it sort of yanked them out.

"I see the way she looks at you," Willard teased. "Course, it's no big deal 'cause all the girls do that."

"Yeah, right," Cody scoffed.

Willard had to smile. Cody was clueless over his good looks and the effect he had on girls, which is probably why the two of them were still best friends.

"There's only one difference," Willard said.

"What's that?"

"I also see the way *you* look at *her*."

Cody glanced down embarrassed. "It's just that she ..." he caught himself and tried again. "It's just that *they* are all alone in that motor home up in the mountains."

"Not exactly." They stopped in front of another gigantic pile of junk. Willard reached in and dug out a laptop computer along with a pair of night-vision goggles.

"Cool," Cody said. "You get those goggles from the Army?"

Willard shook his head. "It's another one of my inventions."

"Uh-oh ..."

"No, listen, these are way cool. Check 'em out." Willard pulled a cable from the pile and began attaching it. "These will let us watch Piper and her brothers wherever they are."

"I hope they work better than your helio-hopper."

"Why's that?"

"'Cause that almost killed us ... twice."

"No," Willard insisted. "These are perfectly safe. You just plug them in, like so ..." He finished attaching the cable to the computer and then the goggles.

"Willard, I don't think—"

"Then you put them on, like so ..." He fitted the goggles over his thick glasses. "Then you enter their email address, like so ..." He typed Zach and Piper's email address into the computer.

"Willard, are you sure—"

"And then finally you turn them on, like so." He flipped a switch on the side of the goggles and waited.

Fortunately, nothing happened.

Cody gave a sigh of relief.

Unfortunately, Willard wasn't done. "Maybe there's a short." He looked to the keyboard. "Maybe ... Wait a minute! Of course! I forgot to hit Enter."

"Willard, I really don't—"

He pressed the key, and the goggles lit up like a Christmas tree. Only it wasn't just the goggles. It was also...

"Willard!" Cody shouted.

The boy's face glowed like a nightlight and his body shook like a bowl of Jell-O on a jack hammer.

"T-t-t-turn i-t-t-t offffff ..." he cried.

"How?" Cody yelled. "Where!?"

"D-d-d-de-leeet-e!" Willard shouted. "Hit-t-t-t D-d-de-lete!"

Cody reached over to the computer and hit the Delete key. Instantly the goggles went off and everything was back to normal.

Well, almost everything...

It seemed Willard's hair was still smoldering. Actually it wasn't so much hair anymore. Now it was more like smoking peach fuzz.

"Are you okay!?" Cody asked.

Willard pulled off his goggles and sighed. "I hate it when that happens."

●

"Boy, you did a number to this baby." The old mechanic slammed shut the engine compartment to the RV.

Zach and Piper traded nervous looks.

"How much is it going to cost?" Zach asked.

"Well first you got your alternator. That's a hundred sixty bucks. Then you got your battery. That's gonna be—"

"Whoa, whoa, whoa." Zach held up his hand. "We don't even have the one sixty."

"Then I'd say you got yourself a problem." The mechanic wiped his hands on an oily rag and limped away. Zach and Piper ran to catch up.

"There must be something you can do," Piper said.

"I can let you use my phone to call your folks."

"I wish it was that easy," she mumbled.

The old man blew his nose into the oily rag, then checked it for results. "If I ain't fixin' it, you ain't leavin' it here," he said.

"Right." Zach looked around, trying to figure out what to do.

"Can we get back to you?" Piper asked.

The old-timer shrugged. "If you ain't got the money, you ain't got the money. 'Less, you're expectin' some sorta miracle."

The word touched off an idea in Zach's mind, and he turned to Elijah. As usual, his little brother was clueless, playing with a caterpillar on a nearby tree.

Zach glanced over to the roadside diner next door. "Can we grab a bite to eat before we give you an answer?"

"Suit yourself. Just don't take too long." The mechanic blew his nose again and checked for results. This time he was more pleased.

●

Mom and Dad entered the dark office. In the shadows, a huge man sat behind his desk. They'd seen him before—felt his chilling power.

"Welcome," he hissed.

Mom shifted, trying to get a better look. But no matter how she moved, his face seemed to stay in shadow, even when light hit it.

"What do you want from us?" Dad demanded. His voice sounded strong, but Mom could tell he was terrified. Who wouldn't be?

"SSSILENCCCE!" the man shouted. "I am the one who assksss the quessstionsss." The room grew very, very still. Ever so slowly, he rose from his desk. "Where isss he?"

"You'll get nothing from us." Dad said.

"Really ...?"

Mom didn't like the man's tone. She liked it even less when he started toward them. Maybe he walked, maybe floated. She couldn't tell in the dark.

"Oh, but I will get sssomething from you," he hissed. "If not your cooperation ... then at leasst their weaknessesss."

"Their weaknesses?" Dad asked.

"Yesss." He arrived and hovered over Mom. She pulled back. "You will tell me their weaknessesss, and I will ussse them."

"What do you mean?" her voice trembled. "Use them for what?"

"Why, to dessstroy them, of courssse." His long fingers shot out and wrapped around her head. She tried to scream but could not find her voice. Suddenly her eyes began to shudder.

"Ssshow me," he hissed. "Ssshow me your oldessst."

Before she could stop herself, thoughts of Zach raced through her mind. Memories.

First there was his weird sense of humor. She remembered the time he was in second grade and he had the entire class believing he came from the strange and mysterious planet, *Whatcha-ma-call-it*. He said he'd been sent as a scout to observe and report what he saw on Earth. If he reported that Earthlings were a kind and generous race (by giving him all their spare change and any cool deserts their mom packed for lunch) then his boss, the mighty warlord of *Whatcha-ma-call-it*, may let them live. If they didn't, well Zach couldn't promise what their fate would be.

"No," the man growled. "Ussselesss." His hands tightened around Mom's head. "Ssshow me sssomething elssse."

Another memory shot through her mind. Suddenly she recalled the time the newspaper called them on the phone.

"Hello?" she answered.

"Hi," the voice on the other end said. "This is the Los Angeles Times."

"The Los Angeles Times?" she had asked.

Of course, that's all Zach heard. In a flash he ran up the stairs, showered and put on his hottest clothes. He was so sure that they were going to do a front page story on him, that he even combed his hair (well, as much as you could comb that type of mess).

It wasn't until he headed back downstairs did he learn that the newspaper just wanted Mom to renew her subscription for another year.

"Worthlesss," the man hissed. "I need sssomething I can ussse to control him with!"

He moved his hands to another part of her head and another memory flashed before her eyes. Only this time there were several images. . . .

Images of him strolling up to pretty girls in the lunch line and introducing himself. Images of him sucking in his stomach and looking all buff when he sauntered past the girl's locker room. Images of him catching a reflection of himself in a store window and smoothing back his hair (if you could call it smoothing) before turning to a nearby girl and piling on the charm.

"Yesss," the evil voice seemed to come from inside her head. "Hisss weaknesss for girlsss. Yesss, I ssshall usssse that." Then he started to laugh. Ugly. Menacing. "Yesss ... yesss ..." His laugh grew louder and louder, filling her head until she collapsed onto the floor and heard nothing at all.

●

"So what do we do?" Piper asked. She and Elijah sat in a booth across from Zach in the diner. "I saw a Help Wanted sign in the window. Maybe I could get a job."

"You don't know how to be a waitress," Zach said.

"I could learn." Zach gave her a snicker and she gave him a look.

"What's that for?" she demanded.

"Sorry," he shrugged, "it's just that you and food, well, you're not always the best of friends."

"Meaning?"

"Remember the last time you tried to fix dinner?"

"Yeah."

"And you served us canned peas?"

Piper felt her ears growing warm. "Alright, so I over-cooked them a little."

"Not if you like chewing on bee-bees," Zach teased.

Piper ears grew a lot warm.

"Or what about that time Dad broke his tooth eating your oatmeal?"

"Okay, so it was a little lumpy."

"And remember the time everybody got sick when you fixed us hamburgers?"

"Not everybody," Piper argued. "You never got sick."

"That's because I fed mine to Molly, the wonder dog."

Piper's eyes widened. "Is that why we had to take her to the vet?"

"That's why we had to take her to the vet *that time*," Zach said. "And that's why they had to pump her stomach. *That time.*"

"You're not going to bring up the other time when you fed her my mac and cheese, are you?"

"The stuff you fried in mustard and ketchup, then smothered in horseradish?" Zach shook his head. "Never."

Piper looked at him suspiciously. "Why not?"

"Because I'm a sensitive kinda guy."

She snorted and blew the hair out of her eyes. Changing the subject, she asked, "So what do you suggest? For making money, I mean?"

"I've got something right here." Zach pulled his hand from his coat pocket and produced a wadded gum wrapper and their life savings of $1.47.

"Great," Piper groaned. "That'll do us a lot of good."

But Zach wasn't listening. Instead, he turned to Elijah. "So what do you think, little guy?"

Elijah looked at the money and smiled.

Zach held it closer.

"What are you doing?" Piper asked.

"Remember back in the RV how he multiplied burgers and fries so we had enough to eat?"

"Yeah . . ."

"So, if he can multiply burgers and fries, he can multiply money."

"Zach . . ."

"What?" He held the money closer. "Come on fella, do your thing."

"Isn't that kind of . . . dishonest?"

"What's dishonest about it?"

At last, Elijah reached for his hand.

"There we go, that's right. Just touch it and . . ."

But instead of taking the money, the boy picked up the wadded gum wrapper.

"No, no, no," Zach said, "the money . . . we need *money*."

Elijah looked at him, grinned, and set the paper on the table.

"No." Zach shook the money in his hand. *"This!"*

Elijah began playing with the wrapper.

"This! Eli, we need more of THIS!"

But Elijah was too busy playing to hear.

Piper covered her mouth, trying not to laugh. Elijah looked up at her. His eyes sparkled like he understood. Maybe he did.

"Hi, there."

Piper turned to see their waitress. She was about Zach's age, with black hair, black clothes, black fingernail polish, and some major black eyeliner. She was definitely Goth, but underneath all that makeup she was probably cute. And by the way she flirted with Zach, she was definitely interested.

"Can I take your order?"

"Yeah," Zach shrugged. "I guess we'll just . . . uh . . ." he glanced down at his money. "We'll just split some fries."

"That's it?"

"All we have is a dollar forty-seven."

"But you're hungry, right?"

"Oh yeah, big time."

"Right." She gave him another smile and started scribbling on her pad. "That's three deluxe burgers, three sides of fries, three milkshakes, and one hot apple turnover."

"No, you don't understand. We can't afford—"

She flipped her hair to the side. "I understand perfectly. And what the boss doesn't know won't hurt him."

"What?"

"It's on the house, big guy."

Zach could only stare. Come to think of it, that's all Piper could do too.

The waitress flashed another smile. "It's the least I can do for a hottie like you." She turned and started off. "I'll be back."

Zach broke into a grin and nodded. "Right. We'll, uh, see you soon."

"Zach," Piper whispered, "we can't do that."

"Why not?" Zach said, still impressed with himself.

"Because she's ripping off the restaurant to feed us."

"Oh well." He shrugged.

"Oh well? That's all you can say?"

"Hey, it's not my fault I'm such a hottie."

Piper rolled her eyes and groaned.

"Hey, it beats green peas, oatmeal, or mac and cheese."

She gave him a slug in the arm.

"Ow."

And then another in the other arm.

"What's that for?" he complained.

"In case I'm not around the next time you're mean."

Chapter Three

A New Friend

"Faster!" Monica yelled. "Faster!"

"Uh, guys?" Bruno called from the backseat.

"I don't understand," Silas said. "The brats were right in front of us!"

"Guys?"

"It's your fault they got away!" Monica yelled. "If Shadow Man finds out, it's your neck, not mine!"

"*Guys!?*"

They both turned and shouted in unison. "*WHAT!?*"

"That hitchhiker back there ... Wasn't he the same homeless guy we saw back in Los Angeles?"

"Bruno," Silas sighed, "that was a hundred miles ago."

"Yeah ..."

"And I've been driving eighty miles an hour the whole time."

"Yeah . . ."

"So there's no way somebody's going to walk faster than I'm driving!"

"Oh, yeah," Bruno giggled. "I get it."

"Good," Silas muttered. "I'm glad."

"Except . . ."

Silas tried to ignore him. He would have succeeded if Bruno hadn't drilled his finger into his back.

"Excuse me . . . Excuse me?"

"What is it, Bruno?"

"What if he was, like, magical or something."

"There is no magic."

"Right . . . but what if he was, like, an angel."

"Bruno . . ."

"Yeah, Silas?"

"Don't be stupid."

"You know I can't help it," said Bruno.

"I know." Silas shook his head. "Believe me, I know."

●

"Sure you don't need some more fries?" The waitress asked. "Maybe some onion rings?"

"No," Zach said, pushing back the remains of his third hamburger. "I'm stuffed."

"A big guy like you needs his nourishment," she said.

The line was so corny, Piper had to look away. Unfortunately, there were more coming.

"You work out, don't you?"

Zach gave a little flex. "You can tell?"

Piper couldn't help snickering. "The only time he works out is when he's reaching for the remote."

Zach shot her a glare.

The waitress laughed. "My name is Ashley. You guys just passing through?"

"Our RV broke down, and we don't have the money to fix it," Zach said. "Unless you know a mechanic who'll work for a dollar forty-seven." Zach chuckled at his little joke, and Ashley laughed like it was the funniest thing she'd ever heard.

Piper glanced away, thinking she might get sick ... and it had nothing to do with the food. That's when she saw the tears in Elijah's eyes. The kid was looking directly at Ashley and getting all misty.

"Hey, little buddy," Piper asked, "you okay?"

Elijah didn't hear. Instead, he slowly reached out and touched Ashley's arm.

"Whoa!" The girl stepped back. "What's with him?"

"He's our little brother," Zach said. "He doesn't mean anything."

"Yeah, well I'm really not into being touched. Kinda creeps me out."

"Really?"

"Long story." Ashley raked her hands through her hair and turned to Piper. "Listen, if you need some cash, why not work here a couple days. I could use a day off, and we really need the help."

"You think they'd hire me?" Piper asked.

"They're so desperate, they'd hire anybody."

Piper nodded and then stopped, not exactly sure it was a compliment.

Ashley motioned to the back. "Go talk to Stan. He's the owner and cook."

"What?" Piper asked. "*Now?*"

"Sure. We're closing up soon. Now's the perfect time."

Piper looked to Zach. "What do you think?"

But Zach was so busy staring at Ashley, he wasn't thinking of anything.

"Zach!"

"What? Oh yeah, sounds good to me."

Piper hesitated. "I really don't—"

"Go ahead," Ashley said. "It'll only take a minute. And while you're doing that," she turned to Zach, "you can walk me home."

"Really?" His voice squeaked like a rusty hinge.

"Well, it's not really home. But it's where we all stay."

"We?" Piper asked.

"Another long story. It's just a few hundred yards from here."

As she spoke, Elijah quietly slipped off the bench and started toward the back door.

"Elijah," Zach called. "Where you going? That's the wrong door!" Elijah didn't turn but arrived at the back door and opened it, patiently waiting.

Ashley chuckled. "Well, I guess you're *both* taking me home."

"Why's that?" Zach asked.

"That's the way to my place." She shrugged. "Strange kid. I wonder how he knew."

Piper and Zach exchanged looks and then answered in unison. "Long story."

●

"Well, that didn't work out so good," Cody said, as he finished brushing the ashes off Willard's bald head.

Willard nodded. "Good thing that was only Plan B."

"Plan B?"

"Yup."

Cody swallowed nervously. "Is there a Plan A?"

Willard smiled an even geekier smile, which always meant trouble. "Knowing where they are isn't going to be all that helpful."

"It isn't?"

"Not really."

Cody wasn't thrilled to ask, but he had little choice. "What *would* be helpful?

Wilbur cranked up his smile to super geek. He motioned for Cody to follow. "I was afraid you were never going to ask."

Cody gave a quiet groan. "And I was afraid I would."

Chapter Four

Real Power

Mom sat on the cell floor with her head on her knees. "I've betrayed him," she softly wept.

Dad called over to her, "Sweetheart ..."

"Our own son. And I've betrayed him." She sniffed. "I don't know who or what that thing is, but I told him."

"You did the best you could."

Somehow his words only made the tears come faster. "I let him read my mind." She looked up, her eyes red and swollen. "I let him know Zach's weaknesses."

At that moment Dad would have given anything to break the chains holding him to the wall, not to be free, just to reach out and hold her.

She buried her face back into her knees. "I'm sorry, Zach ... I'm so sorry."

"Judy." Dad spoke quietly, but firmly. "Listen to me. We don't know who or what that man is, but I think we have a pretty good idea from where he draws his power."

"That's just it." She tried to swallow back her tears. "Zach's only a boy. He could never stand up to that thing on his own."

"And he doesn't have to."

"He doesn't?"

Dad shook his head. "No, he doesn't. We may not be there to help him, at least physically. But there's another way ... and it's more powerful than any other."

"You mean ... are you talking about prayer?"

"That's where the real battles are won or lost. That's where the real power lies."

"But ... he's just a teen."

Dad nodded. "And so was David when he beat Goliath. And Mary. And some of the disciples."

Mom sniffed and slowly started to nod. "Then we better get to work."

"I hear that," Dad said. "And in Zach's case, the sooner the better."

Mom gave a quiet chuckle, which warmed Dad's heart. Then, all alone on the hard stone floor, husband and wife bowed their heads and started to pray.

●

Elijah clung to Zach's hand as they followed Ashley up the wooded trail. The little guy wasn't scared, but something was definitely going on in his head.

"Jason's place is right there." Ashley motioned to a broken-down house in definite need of a paint job.

"Who's Jason?" Zach asked.

"He's this real cool guy who lets a bunch of us stay with him."

"Where are your parents?"

"My stepdad's a junkie who beats me, and my mom's an alcoholic who doesn't care."

"So you ran away?"

Ashley shrugged. "Wouldn't you?"

"I'm ... sorry."

"No biggie," Ashley said. "If I hadn't left them, I'd never have met Jason."

Elijah tugged on Zach's hand. Zach glanced down and saw him motioning for them to head back to the restaurant. But if it came down to spending time with Elijah or Ashley ... well, let's just say there wasn't much competition.

Turning back to Ashley, he asked, "Who exactly is this Jason?"

"Our spiritual advisor."

"Spiritual advisor? You mean like a pastor?"

Ashley broke out laughing. "No way."

"What's so funny? We've got a cool pastor at home."

"Yeah, I'm sure. But Jason, he knows the deeper mysteries, like contacting spirits—that sort of stuff."

Zach tensed. More than once his folks had warned them about fooling around with those types of things. He knew he should probably say something, but Ashley was so beautiful.

Elijah tugged harder. Again Zach ignored him.

At last they reached the porch steps leading to her door.

"Well, here we are." Ashley turned to face Zach just as Elijah yanked on his arm with all of his might.

"What's with him?" she asked.

Zach acted like he hadn't noticed. "Who?"

"Him?"

Again he tried ignoring Elijah, but it's hard to ignore someone when he's yanking your arm out of its socket.

"Is he okay?"

"Oh, yeah," Zach said as casually as possible. "Probably just has to go to the bathroom or something."

Elijah continued yanking and tugging and pulling.

"He looks kinda desperate."

"Yeah, probably," Zach said.

Elijah tucked his legs up and completely hung from Zach's arm.

"There's a restroom back at the restaurant," Ashley said. "I'd hurry and get him there if I were you."

Zach nodded, feeling very much like a human monkey bar.

"So . . ." she turned and headed up the steps. "I guess I'll see you tomorrow."

Zach nodded.

Elijah began swinging back and forth on his arm, like it was a trapeze.

Ashley gave one last smile, mostly out of sympathy. "Good night."

"Good night," Zach answered, still pretending nothing was out of the ordinary.

She opened the door, stepped inside, and quietly closed it behind her.

As soon as it shut, Elijah dropped back to the ground, acting perfectly normal. Zach looked down at him and glared.

Elijah looked up at him and grinned.

Then, without a word, but maybe a little giggle, Elijah turned and skipped back toward the restaurant.

Zach shook his head and started to follow. "I tell you, you're one strange dude, kid."

Cody and Willard rounded another pile of junk and came face-to-face with an old-fashioned telephone booth.

"Here we go," Willard said proudly.

"Here we go, what?" Cody asked.

"Here is the solution to all of our problems."

Cody was afraid to ask, but knew he had no choice. "How will this solve all our problems?"

"Instead of just viewing Piper and her brothers, this will actually send us to visit them. It's my new and improved teleporter machine."

Cody simply stared at him.

"What's wrong?" Willard asked.

"Sounds like you've been watching too many Star Trek reruns."

"No, seriously," Willard said. "You just step inside and punch in Piper's email address."

"And then?"

"And then it will send you to wherever she is."

"Willard?"

"Yes, Cody?"

"Are you taking your medication?"

"Laugh all you want, but there's only one way to find out if it works."

"And that is ..."

"Step inside and try it out."

Cody turned to Willard and gave him one of his world-famous, *are-you-crazy-or-am-I-just-having-a-nightmare* looks.

Unfortunately, it was no nightmare. Instead, it was much worse.

Chapter Five

A New Day

The next morning, after sleeping in the RV, Piper started work in the restaurant. Not only did she not know what she was doing, but she didn't know enough about what she was doing to know she didn't know what she was doing.

Translation: The girl was in trouble.

"Miss!" some fat guy shouted at her for the hundredth time. "I wanted these eggs scrambled!"

Actually, he was lucky to get eggs at all. The first time she had brought him pancakes, the second time three jars of mustard.

"I'm sorry, sir, I'll be right with—"

"Where's my syrup?" an old lady demanded from the next table over.

"And my creamer!" her husband shouted.

"Sorry, I—"

"It's been twenty minutes since I ordered my coffee!" a skinny guy behind them whined.

"Sorry!" She raced to the coffee pot, grabbed it, and headed toward him.

"What about these eggs?"

"I'll be right there." She arrived at the skinny guy's table just in time to hear a familiar voice.

"Hey, Pipe."

She spun around and bumped into Zach and Elijah, sloshing a little of the coffee onto the floor. "Where have you two been?" she asked.

"Lady!" the guy beside her complained. "You spilled coffee on the floor."

"Yes, I know. I'll clean it—"

Zach gave a lazy stretch and answered her question. "I thought we'd sleep in."

"Sleep in?" Piper couldn't believe her ears. "It's—" she turned her wrist to check her watch. Unfortunately, it was the wrist that was connected to the hand that was holding the coffee pot, which explains why the scalding liquid dumped all over the skinny guy's lap.

"Aughhh ..." He jumped up. "Look what you've done! Look what you've done!" He turned and raced for the restroom.

"Sorry!" Piper called after him.

"Where's my syrup?" the old lady shouted.

"Listen," Zach said, "I see you're kinda busy. I'm just going to leave Elijah here and go visit Ashley."

"Zach!" Piper demanded.

"Where's my creamer?"

"Relax," Zach told his sister. "He's got his Bible. You know how he likes lookin' at the pictures and stuff."

"Miss, I want these eggs scrambled!"

Piper turned to her customers, then back to Zach, who was already heading out the door.

"Zach!"

"Could I please have my syrup?"

"Where's my creamer?"

"Sorry." Piper raced back to the counter and grabbed the syrup and creamer. She joined the old couple and apologized as she poured the containers for them. A nice idea ... except the old lady's pancakes were suddenly covered in creamer, while her husband's coffee swam in syrup.

"What are you doing?!" they cried in unision.

Piper was so startled that she leaped back and slipped on the coffee spill, which sent her sliding across the floor...

"Miss, I want these eggs — "

... and landing on the fat man's table, her elbows jabbed in his plate, squirting the yolks from his eggs onto his shirt while she dumped the rest of the creamer and syrup on him.

"MY SHIRT!" He screamed. "LOOK AT MY SHIRT!"

Piper could only stare at his shirt in horror, while at the same time thinking, *Well, at least your eggs are scrambled.*

●

On her best days, Monica Specter was not a happy camper. On her worst days, she was a major terror. And on her worst days without sleep? Don't ask. Let's just say she'd be winning no Miss Congeniality contests.

No one's sure what made her so ill-tempered.

Some say it was growing up as the only girl with six brothers. In most families that would make her a little princess – the sweet, darling girl everybody loved and treated with gentle tenderness.

In Monica's family that meant she was the human guinea pig.

If her brothers wanted to know what would happened if you shoved one hundred fire crackers into the soles of somebody's tennis shoes and lit them, Monica would be the one to find out.

If they wanted to know if an umbrella really worked as a parachute when you jumped off the roof, Monica would provide the answer.

And if they wanted to know what would happen if you stuffed a little girl into an inner tube and rolled her off a 2,000 foot cliff ... well, you probably get the picture.

By the time Monica was seven she learned how to protect herself from any bully.

By the time she was thirteen, the bullies learned how to run for their lives to protect themselves from her.

It's not that she was mean. She was just ... well, she *was* mean.

Real mean.

At the moment she was proving that meanness by screaming at Silas, their driver. "Turn back! "We've missed them! Turn back!"

"What makes you so sure?" Silas said. It had been a while since he'd gotten any sleep and he'd been busy just trying to keep his eyes open.

"The brats were supposed to be rescuing their parents in the mountains!"

"Right."

"So look around you!"

Silas opened his eyes wider. He'd been so tired he hadn't paid much attention to anything the past several hours.

"What do you see?" Monica demanded.

"I know, I know!" Bruno cried eagerly from the back.

"Yes," Monica sighed wearily. "What does Bruno the Brainless see?"

"Sand!" Bruno shouted triumphantly. "Miles and miles of sand."

"Very good. And where do we find miles and miles of sand?"

"Uh ... um ... "

"Come on, Bruno, think. I know it's a new concept, but give it a try."

"I've got it!"

"Yes ..."

"A cat box for giant kitties?"

Monica dropped her head and covered her eyes.

"We're in the desert," Silas said. "We passed over the mountains, and now we're in the desert."

"And what do you suggest we do now?" Monica asked.

"Buy sunscreen!" Bruno exclaimed.

Monica gave a quiet groan.

But Silas knew exactly what to do. Before Monica could blow a major blood vessel, he brought the van to a stop, turned around, and headed back up into the mountains.

●

Zach leaned against the back wall with Ashley. The room was dark except for the single candle that lit a table where three teen boys sat. They were dressed pretty much the same as Ashley—all black with plenty of tattoos and body piercings.

Earlier, Ashley had introduced Zach to them. The skinniest one they called X-Ray. The short one was Stump. And the big one with red hair was called—what else?—Big Red. They seemed nice enough but, unlike Ashley, they were way too cool to smile.

They had set up a board game—something called a Ouija Board—and had just started to play.

"What's it supposed to do?" Zach asked.

"It helps them contact the dead," Ashley whispered.

A chill crept over Zach's body. "The dead?"

"Pretty cool, huh?"

Zach swallowed but did not answer.

"What's wrong?"

"It's just that, well, doesn't the Bible say not to mess with that stuff?"

"Does it?" Ashley asked.

Zach tried to nod, but he wasn't sure how well he pulled it off.

Ashley moved closer and whispered into his ear. "Why do you suppose it says that?" Her presence felt good, and for the moment Zach couldn't think of an answer. Unfortunately, somebody else did.

"Because the Bible is an outdated book of superstitions." The voice was so close that Zach jumped. He turned to see a black-haired skinny guy in his thirties standing beside him. Every square inch of his arms and neck were covered in tattoos.

"Oh, hi, Jason." Ashley leaned past Zach and smiled. "I wondered where you were."

"I see you brought a friend," the man said.

"Yeah," Ashley answered. "Zach, this is our spiritual leader, Jason. And Jason, this is my friend—"

"Zachary," the man spoke slow and soft. "Yes, the driver of the RV. The one helping his younger sister and brother."

If Zach had felt a chill before, he was downright freezing now. "How," he cleared his throat, "how did you know that?"

"Oh, there's a great deal I know about you Zachary—a great, great deal."

Chapter Six

Darkness Closes In

Zach tried his best to stay cool. It would have helped if his heart wasn't pounding a thousand times a second and if he wasn't breathing like he'd just sprinted a dozen miles.

"You don't mind, do you?" Jason asked. "My sensing those things about you?"

Ashley giggled, "I told you he knows stuff."

"But ... how?" Zach managed to croak.

Jason chuckled. "I just talked to Gus, the garage mechanic."

Zach relaxed, but only slightly.

"But you could have learned it other ways too though," Ashley said.

"Oh, yes, I'm frequently in contact with the spirit world," Jason said.

"And that's what he's teaching us," Ashley explained.

"Teaching you?" Zach asked.

Jason merely smiled. "Can I get you guys a beer?"

"Uh, no thanks," Ashley said.

Zach cleared his throat. "None for me."

"Are you sure?"

Zach couldn't tell if Jason was sneering at him or just smiling. "No, I'm good."

"Suit yourself." Jason disappeared into the darkness as Ashley gave another giggle. "Isn't he cool?"

Before Zach could answer, Big Red asked from his seat at the table, "Why isn't it moving?"

"Yeah," Stump complained, "it's never taken this long before."

Zach turned back to Ashley. "What's supposed to happen?"

"Usually that plastic thing they have their hands on starts to move."

"Move?"

"Yeah. See those letters on the board? The spirits move the plastic thing to spell out messages from the dead."

Zach gave a nervous snicker, but Ashley was serious. He glanced around the room, feeling more and more like this was a place he didn't belong.

Jason appeared at their side, sipping a beer.

No, he definitely didn't belong.

"Hey, Jason," Big Red called from the table. "How come it ain't moving?"

"Yeah," Stump said. "Something's stopping it."

"Might be a negative force," Jason said.

"A negative force?" Stump asked.

"Yes, someone who is not open to our powers. Someone afraid to give in to the dark forces."

Zach fidgeted.

Jason continued. "Not only afraid, but actually fighting it. Fighting the darkness."

"Who would do that?" the skinny kid asked.

"Oh, I don't know." Jason turned toward Zach. "Maybe our guest has a clue?"

Zach swallowed. "About what?"

"About who might be stopping our powers? About who in this room is opposed to the powers of darkness?"

By now all eyes were on Zach. And they were not happy eyes.

Again, he tried to swallow, but his mouth was bone dry. "Listen," he coughed. "I better be going. It's getting late." He looked at his watch. It would have been more convincing if he actually wore one, but it seemed a small detail.

"Yes," Jason spoke so softly that it almost sounded like a threat. "I think that would be a fine idea. A very fine idea indeed."

●

Cody watched as Willard grabbed the cord from the back of the telephone booth and looked for an outlet.

"Uh, listen, Willard. I don't want to be a spoilsport, but the last time we tried one of your inventions it almost made me a permanent part of the street pavement."

"Right," Willard said as he pushed aside some old TV sets, a bunch of ancient computers, and pile of electrical junk. "That's the price one pays for being a genius."

"Actually, that's the price *I* pay for you being a genius," Cody said.

"Don't tell me the great Cody is scared," Willard teased.

"Scared?" Cody asked. "No way. Terrified? You bet.

Horrified? Absolutely. Wondering if I should ask my mom and dad to take out a life insurance policy on me? Most likely. But definitely not scared."

"Relax," Willard chuckled. "This will be a piece of cake."

"I'm just saying I'm not crazy about having my body sent through the Internet."

"Ah, here we go." Willard found the outlet and plugged in the cord. Immediately the garage lights dimmed as the phone booth lit up.

Cody continued. "All I'm saying is that maybe we should run a few tests first."

"No problem."

"Really?"

"Sure. Just stand over there at my laptop, and I'll send something to you."

"Like what?"

Willard thought a moment before turning and starting out of the garage.

"Where you going?" Cody shouted.

"I'm going into the garden to grab one of my mom's tomatoes. Turn my laptop back on."

Cody nodded and strolled over to Willard's combination laptop/hair remover. Moments later, Willard returned and placed a tomato on the floor of the phone booth.

"Now turn the speakers up nice and loud," Willard said.

Cody reached over to the laptop and turned the volume up to high.

"You ready?" Willard called.

Cody looked at the laptop, took a step back just to be safe, and shouted, "Ready."

Willard punched a series of buttons on the phone, quickly stepped out of the booth, and shut the door. "Stand by!"

The booth started shaking. Then rattling. Then it started to make strange sounds:

GIRRR-GIRRR-GIRRR

like a coffee grinder gone berserk. Then it started another sound:

DING-DING-DING-DING

like a railroad crossing on too much caffeine. And, finally, it began the ever popular sound of a:

KERUGACHA-KERUGACHA-KERUGACHA.

cement mixer stuck on high.

All of this as the light inside grew brighter and brighter. Suddenly there were more sparks than the Fourth of July and:

POP!

it was all over. (Well, except for the cloud of smoke).

And, there, in front of the computer and speakers, sat a lovely, ripe tomato.

Well sort of...

The good news was the tomato had transported across the Internet. The bad news was it had transported into a pile of steaming ketchup.

"Uh, Willard?"

The pudgy inventor raced toward him in excitement. "How'd we do?"

"You might want to make a couple adjustments."

●

Ashley tried to follow Zach outside, but Jason blocked her. "I'd like to see you in my office a moment."

"I should really check on Zach and—"

"This *is* about Zachary."

Ashley looked up into his coal-black eyes. The man was deadly serious. And when he got that way, she knew it was best not to argue. She'd seen the way he'd humiliated other kids that gave him trouble. Sometimes he made fun of them in front of the entire group. Sometimes he gave them the worst jobs, like cleaning the toilet. And sometimes he completely ignored them like they weren't even there – for days or even weeks.

Without a word, the two of them walked toward his office and entered.

Since Jason liked darkness, there were no lights in the room, and the drapes were drawn to keep out the sun. He pulled up a chair at the end of a long table and sat. "So ... tell me *all* you know about Zachary."

Ashley shrugged. "There really isn't much to tell. He's a nice guy, and he's got a sister and a strange little brother."

"Yes," Jason nodded and lit up a cigarette. "The brother. Tell me about the brother."

"I can't really explain it. It's like there's something different about him. Like he's really simple but at the same time he seems to know stuff."

Jason remained sitting in the dark for a long moment. It was impossible to see his face; only the glow from his cigarette. Finally, he spoke.

"I think it is time to elevate you, my dear."

"Elevate me?" she asked.

"The spirits have confirmed to me that you are very special."

"Me?" Ashley's heart began to race. Wasn't that the whole reason she'd been attracted to Jason and his group in the first place? No one else accepted her, but his group did. Not only accepted her, but there was always the hint that she just might have special powers.

And now ... wasn't that exactly what Jason was saying?

"Yes," he whispered. "Very, very special."

"How—" She could barely find her voice. "How so?"

"You have the ability to draw people ... to lead them to us for enlightenment."

"Like who? I don't know anybody."

"You know Zachary. He is special, don't you agree?"

Ashley nodded, almost smiling. He was special ... at least to her.

Jason continued, "He will draw other special people—like his sister and, most importantly, his little brother."

Ashley continued to stare at the glowing cigarette.

"Tell him he is invited to our séance this afternoon."

"But, you saw how freaked he was with the—"

"Yes ... and I'm afraid I didn't help. Please apologize to him for me. And tell him I am specifically holding the event in his honor."

"And if he still doesn't want to come?"

"You'll see to it that he does."

"But, I don't want to pressure him. I mean if he feels uneasy, maybe—"

Jason pounded the table. "You'll see to it that he does!"

The outburst shocked Ashley. She wasn't sure what to do. But Jason's voice quickly softened, becoming as quiet and mysterious as it always was. "That is your destiny, my dear. Your high calling. That is why you have been chosen."

Almost against her will, Ashley felt herself beginning

to nod. Part of it was the excitement of being so pecial. Part of it was fear of what would happen if she disobeyed.

Chapter Seven

A Strange Customer

It had been a long, tiring morning as Silas retraced their route back up the mountain road. They stopped at every turnout and rest stop along the way. The kids' RV had to be somewhere.

It wasn't any easier with Bruno the Belching Machine sitting in the back. Apparently he'd eaten something that didn't agree with him. Silas couldn't imagine what. It was just the usual five double cheeseburgers, four greasy tacos, a couple of sides of onion rings, three apple turnovers, and one giant econo Big Swallow hold the ice.

And if all his burping and belching wasn't enough, there was the little call Monica got from Shadow Man.

"You lossst them, didn't you?" he hissed through her cell phone.

Monica's face twitched nervously. It's not that she was afraid to talk to the Shadow Man. She was terrified. Come to think of it, so was everybody else in the van. It wasn't the *shadow* part of his name that scared them. It was the *man* part.

They just weren't sure if it was true.

There were parts of him that were like a man. I mean you could see him and everything. And there was his need to sleep and eat ... and eat ... and eat.

But there were other things ... like the way you could never quite see his face. The way he always seemed to be in shadows even on sunny days.

And there was something else ...

The way he always knew what others were thinking. Or what they were feeling. Sometimes, even from a great distance, he knew what they were doing. Definitely weird. In fact, on the Freaky Scale of 1-10, he was definitely an 11. Someone whose good side you wanted to stay on. If such a thing was ever possible.

"The bratsss are at a truck sssstop," he hissed. "I sssee a garage and diner."

Monica swallowed. "Sir, are you sure? Because, we've been—"

"Sssilenccce!"

Monica closed her mouth.

"You will find the little boy, and you will bring him to me!"

"What about the others—the brother and sister?"

"They are of no interessst. Dissspossse of them as you sssee fit."

"Yes, sir." Monica waited until the man hung up and then, with shaking hands, closed her phone.

"What did he say?" Silas asked.

"What do you think he said?" she snapped. Talk-

ing to the Shadow Man always put her a little on edge.
"Find them!"

Another hour had passed before Silas slowed the
van.

"Why are we stopping?" Monica demanded.

"We're coming up to where we first lost them."

"How can you tell?"

Silas pointed ahead. "There's the railing we bounced
off of when I almost hit that guy."

"Let me see!" Bruno leaned forward from the seat
behind them. Unfortunately, he leaned just a little too
far, just a little too fast, considering how queasy his
stomach was. Which would explain his sudden...

BLAAHH!

as he threw up all over Silas and Monica.

Of course Monica did her usual screeching and
name-calling.

Silas, on the other hand, was too busy jerking away
and yanking the steering wheel. No problem, except that
he threw the van completely out of control. So, just like
old times, the vehicle skidded and the tires squealed.

"Look out!" Monica shouted.

"I got it!" Silas yelled.

BLAAAAHHHH!

Bruno threw up again.

They slammed into the exact same railing as before.
And, for a moment, it looked like they were going over
the cliff. But Silas fought the wheel, and after a few
more skids, squeals (and screechings from Monica), he
regained control.

The good news was they had once again missed seeing the garage and the diner.

The bad news was, Bruno still had a little food left
in his—

BLAAAAAAHHHHHH!
Never mind, it's gone now.

●

If Piper thought the breakfast folks were demanding, they were nothing compared to the lunch crowd. The place was packed with twice as many customers, who were twice as rude.

"Where's Ashley?" Piper called to Stan, her boss. He was cooking at the grill. "When does she come in?"

"Not till tomorrow."

"Tomorrow!? You mean I'm all by myself?"

"Don't worry, kid." He set out three more hamburger platters for her. "You're doing great."

Piper grabbed the platters and turned. Unfortunately, they were hot, and one slipped from her hands. It crashed to the floor, sending hamburger, fries, and catsup in all directions. Of course, everyone stopped and stared. And, of course, Piper felt her ears turning their usual beet red.

Stooping down to clean the mess, she muttered, "This is obviously a new definition of 'doing great.'"

When she rose, she saw that a gray-haired gentleman had entered and was sitting next to Elijah. He was pointing something out in the Bible, and Elijah was nodding, eagerly listening.

Feeling a surge of panic, Piper made a beeline past the other customers to her brother's table. When she arrived she asked, none too politely, "May I help you?"

The man looked up, and Piper caught her breath. "Aren't you ... aren't you the guy who had the heart attack in Pasadena?"

The man smiled kindly. "Lots of folks mistake me for other people."

"Yes, but—"

"I guess I just have one of those faces."

Piper frowned, not entirely convinced. She wasn't sure how to ask the man to leave her brother alone, especially since Elijah was so excited over what they were studying. So she tried another approach. "Can I get you something?"

"No, thank you." He pointed to the cherry pie and cup of coffee in front of him. "This should do me."

Piper's frown deepened. "But I ... I didn't wait on you."

The man's grin broadened. "Maybe you just don't remember."

"No, I—"

"Actually, I think you're a lot better waitress than you give yourself credit for."

"Yeah, right." She rolled her eyes and turned to the customers behind her. "Tell that to all these—"

She came to a stop. To her amazement, every customer had their food. Not only that, but they were all perfectly content.

Her mouth dropped open as she slowly turned to the man.

But he was back in the book studying with Elijah.

"How ... how ..."

He looked up. "I see your little brother likes to read the Bible."

"Yes," she answered numbly. "He likes Revelation."

"Especially Revelation 11," the old-timer acknowledged.

"Revelation 11?"

"The passage about the two prophets."

Piper scowled, trying to remember. "You mean the two guys that come out of heaven?"

"Not exactly," he corrected.

"What do you mean?" Piper asked.

"I mean prophets usually start off as little boys, don't they?"

"Miss," a customer politely called.

Reluctantly, Piper turned to a young mother.

"May I have a refill on my iced tea? When you have the time, I mean?"

"Oh, sure." Piper turned back to the gentleman. "I, uh, have to get back to work."

"Certainly," he smiled.

With her mind spinning, Piper headed over to the iced tea pitcher. She heard the little bell above the door ring and turned to see Zach enter. He looked a little tired and a lot pale. She picked up the pitcher and moved to refill the young mother's glass.

"Thanks," the woman said.

Piper nodded and looked back to Elijah's table just as Zach sat down beside him.

The gray-haired gentleman was nowhere to be found.

●

Dad turned to Mom in the dark cell. They'd been praying off and on throughout the night and into the morning. It was harder work than either had expected.

"How are you doing, sweetheart?" he asked.

"Fine," she said. "It's just—"

"Just what?"

"I feel like all I'm doing is asking for the same thing over and over again—for the children's protection, for their safety, that we get out of here and help them."

Dad nodded. "I know what you mean."

"It seems like there should be more."

"More?"

"More than just asking the same thing over and over again."

Dad thought a moment then answered. "Maybe there is."

"What do you mean?"

"Instead of just asking ... maybe we should also be worshipping."

"What, *here? Now?*"

"God's still in control, right? Whatever happens, he still deserves our love."

"Right."

"So maybe part of our prayers should also be worship."

"Like a song or something?

"I know it sounds crazy, especially in a place like this, but ..." He dropped off, feeling a little embarrassed. But when he turned to Mom, he saw she was starting to nod.

"Maybe ... maybe you have a point."

He shrugged. "I mean that's what they did in the Bible, remember? Even when they were thrown in jail, they sang songs to God."

"I'd almost forgotten."

There was a long moment's silence. Then, in the dark, Mom started to hum.

Dad recognized the tune immediately. It was one of his wife's favorites. He smiled as the humming turned into words:

Amazing grace, how sweet the sound
That saved a wretch like me ...
Eventually he joined in.
I once was lost, but now I'm found,
Was blind but now I see.

Together, their voices grew louder and louder. And, although they were tired and exhausted, they soon filled the room with their singing.

Chapter Eight

Conflicts Grow

"Zach . . ."

Zach looked up as Ashley approached their table. "Can I talk to you a moment?"

"Oh, hi. Sure." He noticed Elijah reaching out to her. So did Ashley.

"Outside?" she said. "Alone?"

Zach nodded and stood. "I'll be right back, little buddy."

Elijah nodded and sadly watched as Zach followed Ashley to the door.

Once they were outside in the afternoon sun, she turned to Zach. "Look, I'm really sorry about what happened back there."

"No, that's okay." He shrugged. "It was my fault. I should never have gone in the first place."

"What do you mean?"

"I mean there's some bad stuff going on up there."

"Just because you don't understand it, doesn't make it bad."

Zach nodded. "It's just that the Bible says pretty strong things against doing that kind of —"

"That's why Jason wants you to come back," Ashley interrupted.

"Come back?"

"Yeah. He wanted me to apologize for him for making you feel so bad."

"He said that?"

"He thinks you're real special and that you deserve to be treated a lot better."

Zach arched an eyebrow. Maybe this Jason wasn't such a bad guy, after all.

Ashley took a step closer. "He wanted you to better understand what we're about."

Zach frowned.

"I mean," she moved closer, "how do you know something's wrong, if you don't really know what it is?" She looked up at him with those big, beautiful eyes.

He swallowed.

"You know," she reached out and took his hand. "He thinks you and me ... he thinks we both have potential."

Zach's voice cracked. "Potential?"

She smiled and nodded. "He's going to do something special in your honor, and all he wants is for you to come back so he can show you." She glanced down and then looked back up with those incredible eyes. "That's all I want too."

"Well ..." Zach cleared his throat. Most of him knew that he shouldn't. But there was another part that figured it wouldn't hurt. Besides, like she said, how could he know something was wrong, if he really didn't understand it? He cleared his throat again. "We'll, uh, we'll see."

"Great!" She rose up on her toes and gave him a peck on the cheek. "We'll see you at five o'clock."

Before he could answer, she turned and started up the hill.

"Ashley . . ."

She turned and flashed him that killer smile. "Don't be late."

Zach wanted to say something, to tell her not to get her hopes up. But at the moment, he couldn't think of any words.

●

It was late afternoon by the time Piper finally got her lunch break. She dragged herself with Zach over to the RV to see what progress the mechanic had made.

"It's the weirdest thing," the grizzly old guy said. "I fired her up 'bout an hour ago, and she ran like a top."

Zach and Piper exchanged looks and then glanced over to Elijah, who was playing with a ladybug on a bush.

Zach turned back to the mechanic. "What exactly do you mean?"

"I mean, as far as I can tell, there ain't nothin' wrong with your vehicle . . . at least now."

Piper's excitement grew. "You're saying it runs?"

"As good as new."

"You mean, we can just go?"

"Any time you want. Now if you'll excuse me, I got some real work to get to." With that, the old man limped off.

Piper turned to Zach and practically squealed. "Can you believe it? We can leave! I don't have to work at that place anymore! We can get out of here now!"

Zach nodded.

She turned toward the diner and then back to Zach. "I'll finish my shift, though. I owe Stan that much. But afterward, we can get out of here and—"

She came to a stop. Zach was shaking his head.

"What's wrong?" she asked.

"There's something I gotta do first."

"What do you mean?"

"I promised Ashley I'd go back to Jason's."

"Jason's?!"

He glanced to the ground. "Yeah."

"You said they were messing with spirits and witchcraft and stuff."

"They are."

"But—"

"But Ashley's different. I think I can help her."

"Why? 'Cause she's pretty and thinks you're cool?"

He gave her a scowl. "Get real."

"What then?"

"She's just trying to find herself and be liked."

"So?"

"So she's going to the wrong place for it."

Piper blew the hair out of her eyes. "And what are you going to do, point her to the right place?"

He shrugged. "I should at least try."

Piper couldn't believe her ears. She put her hands on her hips. "What are you saying? You're going to tell her about God and stuff?"

Another shrug. "I'd be a jerk if I didn't."

Piper's anger grew. She couldn't tell if he really wanted to help the girl or if he really liked her. Either way, going back to that house was stupid. And dangerous.

"Hey Piper!" She turned to the diner. Stan stood at the door calling after her. "Break time's over, girl!"

She turned to Zach who was still staring at the ground.

"Piper!"

She called back to Stan. "All right! I'll be right there!" She turned to Zach. "Going back there is stupid, real stupid."

He nodded. "Yeah, probably."

"And you're still going to do it?"

It seemed like forever before he looked up. When he did, she saw his eyes were shiny with emotion. "What else ..." His voice caught and he tried again. "What else can I do?"

●

Jason's house was packed. Zach counted at least a dozen kids, all teens. But only five of them had been chosen to sit at the round table with Jason.

As the guests of honor, two of the chosen ones were Ashley and Zach.

Jason called out to Big Red. "If you will, pull the drapes, please?"

The big guy obeyed, and the room instantly fell into darkness. Now it was lit only by a single candle on the table. The good news was there was no Ouija Board before them. The bad news was ... well, Zach was about to find out.

"Place your hands on the table," Jason ordered. "Close your eyes and concentrate. It is time for us to commune with the other side."

"A séance?" Zach whispered to Ashley. "You didn't say we were going to have a séance!"

She whispered back. "I told you we speak to departed spirits."

Zach shook his head.

"What?" Ashley asked.

"Those aren't dead spirits."

"What makes you the expert?"

"I'm not. But the Bible says once we die we all go to face God."

"If they're not dead spirits, what are they?"

Zach swallowed, took a breath and answered. "Demons."

"Ashley? Zachary?" Although Jason's voice was quiet and smooth, his eyes flashed intensely. "You're not concentrating."

Zach's heart pounded in his chest. He knew what he should do, but with Ashley there, with all the kids standing around staring at him...

Jason's eyes narrowed. "Is there a problem, Zachary?"

Zach took a deep breath. And then another. Finally, with trembling legs, he rose to his feet.

Chapter Nine

Deception

Before Zach could speak, Jason closed his eyes and shouted. "Oh, spirit, we beseech you! We beseech you to speak! We beseech—"

Zach took another breath.

"We beseech you, speak!"

Finally, Zach answered. "This isn't right." But he could barely be heard.

"Spirit, we beseech you—"

"I said this isn't—"

Jason's head snapped back. Everyone gasped and the room fell strangely silent. Then, ever so quietly, Jason began to speak. But it wasn't his voice. It was someone, some*thing*, entirely different.

"I wisssh to sssspeak to Zzzachary."

Zach stiffened. All eyes in the room turned to him as people started to murmur.

"Sssilence!" the voice hissed. "Zzzachary. Do you hear me?"

Ashley looked up to Zach, "Answer him," she whispered. "He's calling you."

Zach turned to Jason. "Who . . . who are you? What do you want?"

"I have a messsage from your mother."

Zach's heart skipped a beat. "What about my mother?"

"Your parentsss. They are trapped. Held sssomewhere. Yesss?"

Zach gave no answer. Part of him was dying to know what the voice knew. But the other part knew the voice was a spirit. A demon. Memories rushed in. Memories of Bible stories where Jesus ran into just such creatures. And memories of the authority he had over them.

"You mussst hurry," the voice continued. "Ressscue them. Ressscue them before it isss too—"

Zach had enough. "Stop it!" he ordered.

"You mussst hurry and—"

"I command you to stop!"

Instantly, the voice fell silent.

Zach looked on, breathless and a little surprised.

Jason's mouth began to contort. Every so slowly he looked to Zach, his lips twisting into a snarl.

Zach took a shaky breath and continued. "I order you to—"

"Sssilencccce!" Jason roared. "You have no authority over me!"

Zach's mind raced. What happened? Maybe it was true. Maybe he didn't have authority. Maybe the demons didn't have to obey. But how could that be? Whenever Jesus ordered them in the Bible, they had to—

And then he had it. Of course! What was he thinking? It wasn't *Zach's* authority they had to obey. With the added knowledge, he took another breath and tried again. "By the authority of *Jesus Christ*, I order you to stop talking!"

Jason glared at him and opened his mouth. But instead of words, there was only a choking sound—like he was trying to speak, but couldn't.

Zach reached down for Ashley's hand. "Let's get out of here."

She looked up frightened, confused. "What have you done to him?!"

Zach turned back to Jason as the man continued to gurgle and choke. He looked back to Ashley. "Come on."

"You're hurting him!"

"I'm not—"

"You're not letting him talk!"

Zach tried to explain. "It's not me."

"You're ruining it!"

"Ash—"

"You're ruining everything!"

"Ashley ..."

"Go!" Her voice cracked with emotion. "Get out of here!

Zach looked back to Jason and then to the surrounding kids who glared at him. Then back to Ashley.

Her eyes flashed in hurt and anger. "I said go!"

As much as he wanted to help, it was clear she didn't want it.

"Go!" She was beginning to cry. "Get out of here! Go!"

Finally, sadly, Zach turned and started toward the door.

●

Mom and Dad finished another song.

Originally, when they had first started, there was no difference. The situation was the same, the cell was the same, their fear was the same. But gradually, as they started the second or third song, they began to feel different. A type of peace settled over them. It was as if they sensed God was in charge. Everything else was exactly the same. The only thing that had changed was them.

And, at least for now, that was enough.

They'd barely finished the last song before they heard the rattling of keys.

"Mike!" Mom pressed against the wall, frightened.

The door creaked open, and a light flooded in. A figure stepped into the doorway. It was impossible to see his face because of the brightness behind him.

"Who are you?" Dad demanded. "What do you want?"

Without a word, the figure entered the cell and stooped down. He looked familiar, but Dad couldn't quite place him. "What do you want?" Dad repeated.

The man produced a key and quickly unlocked the chains to Dad's feet and hands. Silently, he moved to Mom and unlocked her chains.

"We're not going back to that monster!" Dad said. "There's no way, we're—"

"Your work here is finished," the man said quietly.

"Our ... *work*?" Dad asked.

The figure rose. "Your prayers have been answered."

"What do you mean?" Mom said.

The figure stepped out of the room and pointed. "Follow this hallway to the exit. You will find that the door is unlocked. One hundred and fifty yards away, in the woods, you will discover your vehicle."

Dad rose to his feet. "I don't understand."

"Your prayers have been answered." With that, the figure turned and disappeared down the hall.

●

Cody scooped up the tomato in front of the computer. He looked it over and over, first one way, then another, searching for the slightest problem. There was none. The tomato was perfect. The test was a success.

"What did I tell you?" Willard gloated. "It just took a few minor adjustments. Now it's time for us to take the plunge."

"Not so fast," Cody said.

"Now what?"

"It's one thing for it to work with vegetables. What about animals?"

"Meaning?"

"Meaning we're animals, not vegetables. Meaning we have to make sure it's safe for animals."

"Oh, brother," Willard sighed.

"Better safe than sorry," Cody said.

"All right, hang on." Willard waddled out and returned a minute later. In his hand he held two cages. One contained a hamster, the other a parakeet. "Which one do you want to send?" he asked.

"How 'bout both?" Cody said.

"Both?"

"There'll be two of us. Let's send two of them."

"Why are you so picky?" Willard demanded.

"I'm not picky," Cody said, "I just got this thing about living."

"All right, all right," Willard sighed. "We'll do another test, just to keep you happy. " He opened the phone booth and set both cages inside. Once again he pressed a series of numbers on the keyboard, shut the door, and waited as the sound and light show began.

First there was the:

GIRRR-GIRRR-GIRRR-ing

Next came the:

DING-DING-DING-ing

And, last but not least, came the:

KERUGACHA-KERUGACHA-KERUGACHA

After the expected sparks, flashes, and ever-popular:

POP!

both animals appeared in front of the computer's speakers. It was another success.

Well, almost...

"How'd we do?" Willard asked, heading over to join Cody.

Cody stared at the two cages, blinking. The parakeet still had her parakeet body, only she no longer had wings. Worse than that, instead of her head, she now had the hamster's head. And the hamster? Not only did he have the parakeet's head, but he was also the proud owner of two parakeet wings.

"A little more tweaking?" Cody suggested.

Willard nodded. "A little more tweaking."

●

"There it is!" Monica shouted.

They had turned back again. And this time, to their right, was a diner and a small gas station. And parked directly beside the station was the kids' motor home.

Silas turned the van and brought it to a stop beside the RV.

"I don't see no lights inside," Bruno complained.

Monica answered, "They're obviously over in that diner."

"Are we gonna go in and grab 'em?" Bruno asked hopefully.

Monica shook her head. "Too many witnesses. We have to wait till they come out."

"And then we grab 'em!" Bruno giggled in glee.
"Yes my sweet, dumb pet. Then we grab them."

Chapter Ten

Tensions Build

"You're so judgmental!"

Ashley had come from Jason's to give Zach a good piece of her mind. Now they sat across from one another in the diner having a major argument.

"Ashley, you know what was going on in there was evil. I felt it. You felt it."

"Just because it doesn't fit into your neat little world doesn't make it wrong."

"It's not my world, Ashley. It's God's. He's the one who makes the rules, and he's the one who says messing with spirits is wrong. Not only wrong, but dangerous."

"Stop it!" She covered her ears. "Will you just stop with the preaching!"

"I can't change the truth. Jason's bad news and—"

"Stop it!"

Those sitting closest to them turned and looked. It hurt Zach to see her so torn up, but he didn't know what else to do. Finally he reached across the table and took her hand. "I'm only trying to help—"

"Well maybe you should stop trying."

"What?"

She pulled her hand away. "Maybe I'm not worth it. You ever think about that? Maybe Jason and his buddies are all I deserve."

"Ash—"

"You, your sister, and your weird little brother come breezing in with all your fancy God talk, and then you just up and leave."

"You're mad 'cause we're going?"

"No, I think you should go. And the sooner the better." She rose to her feet, tears filling her eyes.

"What are you saying?" he asked.

She took a deep breath and answered. "I'm saying good-bye, Zach. I don't want to see you. I don't want to hear from you.

"How can you say that?"

She wiped her face and turned toward the back door.

"Ashley . . ." He reached for her arm, but she shook it loose. She started for the door when Piper suddenly appeared from the kitchen. She was out of her uniform and holding Elijah's hand.

Ashley was in no mood for another confrontation, so she spun around and headed for the front door instead.

"Ashley," Zach called after her.

She walked faster.

"Ashley!"

She reached the front of the diner, threw open the door, and broke into a run.

Zach could only stare after her, speechless.

Piper arrived at the table and said, "Don't tell me you're just going to stand there."

He turned to her. "What else can I—"

"You really are clueless, aren't you?"

"What?"

"Go after her!"

"But she just said—"

Piper shook her head in disgust and looked down at Elijah. "Is every guy this ignorant about girls?"

Elijah grinned, shrugged, and then nodded.

She looked back to Zach, who remained standing, still puzzled.

"Go," she motioned him toward the door. "Go, go, go!"

And for once in his life Zach took his little sister's advice.

●

"There's the oldest!" Monica pointed toward the diner as Zach raced out the door. "Follow him!"

Silas and Bruno leaped into action.

Well, actually Silas did the leaping. Bruno had a bit more trouble.

"Uh . . . I can't get my seatbelt undone."

Monica turned back to him and glared. "What?!"

"It's stuck or somethin'."

"No way," Silas said. He opened Bruno's door and reached for the buckle. "You probably just forgot how to use it."

"I'm not that stupid," Bruno pouted. "You showed me how this afternoon."

Silas gave the buckle a tug, but it wouldn't budge.

"See." Bruno brightened. "I told you."

"Fools!" Monica reached back to the buckle. "Do I have to do everything myself!?"

She gave the buckle a pull. Nothing. She pulled harder. Still nothing. Then she pulled with all of her might . . . again and again and again, until the entire van started rocking back and forth.

"Uh, Monica . . ."

"Not now, Bruno." She continued yanking and the van continued rocking.

"I think I'm going to get sick."

"Don't you dare," Monica warned.

"Okay," Bruno said. "Uh, Monica?"

"What now!?"

BLAAAAAAAAA!

●

Mom and Dad followed the hallway until they came to a sharp corner. Carefully, Dad peered around it. There was the exit fifteen feet away—a clear shot.

Well, except for the two men blocking the door.

Dad pulled back and whispered to Mom. "There are guards."

"How are we going to get past them?"

"I don't know, I—"

He was interrupted by a familiar voice. He peeked around the corner and saw the man who had unlocked their chains. He was talking with the guards smoothly, almost hypnotically.

Dad watched as the guards lowered their rifles. Their eyes were open but just a little glazed as they slowly turned and started down the hallway toward him.

He pulled back and flattened against the wall, motioning Mom to do the same.

She did, just as they rounded the corner.

Mom and Dad each held their breath, afraid to move a muscle.

But the trio continued right on past, so close the parents could have reached out and touched them. Yet for some reason the guards didn't see them. Instead they just kept walking by with that glassy look in their eyes.

Dad waited until they were a dozen feet away before he grabbed Mom's hand. "Come on," he whispered, "let's go!"

They raced for the door and pushed it open. A shrill alarm started blasting as they ran out into the pitch-black woods. Behind them they heard shouting.

There was no turning back now.

●

Willard had run several more tests. Soon the parakeet and hamster began arriving exactly as they should—all body parts intact and on the right bodies.

That was the good news.

Unfortunately, there was some bad.

"Okay, Cody, we're next."

Cody gave a nervous swallow. "Are you sure it's ready?"

"Yup. I've run every test I can run. And then some. We're all ready to go."

Cody looked at the phone booth, then to Willard, then to the hamster and parakeet, then back to the phone booth.

With nothing left to do, he gave another swallow.

●

"Ashley ... Ashley!" By the time Zach caught up to her, she was almost at Jason's porch.

She turned, tears streaming down her face. "Leave

me alone," she cried. "Go back to your perfect little life and leave me alone!"

"Ashley, please ..." He grabbed her arm. "You don't belong here. Not with these people."

"Right," she sniffed. "I should go back to a drunk mom and a crazy stepdad."

"Yes. I mean no. I mean if you go back, there are people who can help you."

"Yeah, right."

"I'm serious. You don't have to do it on your own. And you sure don't have to be with people like Jason."

"But he accepts me," she choked out the words, "just the way I am. And, and he says I'm special."

"You are special. You're God's child."

"Puleease," she said with scorn.

"You are! And he'd do anything for you."

"Right, that's why he gave me a couple of loser parents."

Zach shook his head. "I don't have an answer for that. But I do know he gave you the most important thing he had."

"What's that?"

"His life. When he died on that cross."

Ashley snorted in disgust.

"I'm serious. When Jesus was up on that cross dying for all the wrong you and I did ... at that moment, he considered us way more important than his life. Think of that. God thought you were more valuable than his own life."

Ashley tried wiping away her tears, but they came faster. Even if she wanted to answer, she couldn't.

Unsure what to do, Zach pulled her into his arms. She didn't resist. As he held her, he felt her body tremble. She was sobbing. How long they stayed that way, he didn't know. But he did know when the door opened and light spilled on them from inside the house.

"Well, well, lookie here." Jason walked onto the porch. Some of the kids joined him. "It's the God squad."

Zach stepped forward. "It's over, Jason."

"And what is that?"

"Ashley's not staying with you any longer."

"Oh really," Jason sneered. "Is that true, my dear?"

Ashley hesitated.

"Is it!?"

Finally she wiped her face and gave a little nod.

"Yes, well, we'll see about that." Turning to the kids on either side of him, he gave the order:

"Grab them!"

Chapter Eleven

Confrontation

Before Zach could move they were on him—Stump, X-Ray, and Big Red.

"Let go of him!" Ashley shouted. "Let—"

Someone hit the side of Zach's head and for moment he started to lose consciousness—until he heard Ashley scream. They were attacking her too!

That was all he needed to stay awake and fight back.

He landed a powerful punch into Big Red's stomach, doubling him over.

One of Jason's thugs down. Two to go.

He caught a glimpse of Ashley being dragged up the porch steps by Stump. "NO!" she screamed. "LET GO OF ME!"

X-Ray, the tall skinny kid, grabbed Zach's arms and twisted them behind his back so he couldn't move them. But Zach could move his feet. He kicked his right foot back and slammed it into the kid's knee.

"Augh!" X-Ray cried.

But Zach wasn't done. Using the same foot, he scraped it down the boy's shin, hopefully taking off a layer of skin, and then stomped his heel on top of the kid's foot.

X-Ray let go and grabbed his foot. "AUGHHH!"

Two down.

Letting go of Ashley, Stump leaped on Zach's back and wrapped his arms around his throat. Zach put his right fist into his left hand and jerked his elbow into the kid's stomach.

"Oaff!"

Three down!

He turned toward Ashley just as Jason dragged her through the door. But Zach had no sooner taken a step toward her when his head exploded in pain. Suddenly his legs had no strength, and he dropped to his knees. He looked up and saw Big Red standing over him holding a board.

Zach fell forward, unable to stop himself. He was unconscious before he hit the ground.

●

The alarm continued to sound as Mom and Dad raced through the woods. The undergrowth grabbed their legs, and branches kept slapping their faces. Now, if they only knew where they were going.

"I don't see a thing." Mom gasped for breath.

"He said the Jeep was just ahead!"

"But there's no road! Not even a trail!"

Back at the compound they heard the opening of a gate and the barking of dogs.

"We'll never make it!" Mom yelled.

The same thought shot through Dad's mind, but he pushed it aside. He had to be positive. He had to be brave. Not just for his wife, but also for the kids.

"What's that?" he asked.

"Where?"

"Just ahead, up on the ridge?"

They squinted into the dark. Maybe it was the Jeep, maybe it wasn't. There was only one way to find out.

"Let's go!" Dad shouted. "Up on the ridge?"

They squinted into the dark. Maybe it was the Jeep, maybe it wasn't. There was only one way to find out.

"Let's go!" Dad shouted.

The raced up the hill, fighting through the brush and branches. Mom stumbled once, then again, nearly falling. But Dad was there to pull her to her feet.

"You okay?" he asked.

She nodded, but had to stop to catch her breath. So did Dad. They leaned over, their hands on their knees, breathing in the cold, sharp air. In the distance, the barking grew louder, closer.

He turned to her. "You ready?"

Still breathing too hard to answer, she nodded.

He grabbed her hand and they started back up the hill. In less than a minute they reached the top. But to their dismay there was no Jeep. Instead, they discovered a rusted-out camping trailer. "Michael," his wife cried, "what do we do?"

"I don't know. The man said it was just up—"

"Look!" She pointed to a dirty window of the camper. Through the dirt, in clear sharp lines, someone had drawn an arrow pointing to the right.

Dad followed it and—"There it is!" he shouted. He pointed to the Jeep parked less than fifty yards away. "Let's go!"

They sucked in another breath and resumed running.

●

"Are you ready?" Willard asked.

Cody stared at the phone booth. He wanted to nod, but he'd never been a big fan of suicide.

"I'll take that as a yes." Willard opened the door.

Reluctantly, Cody stepped in and Willard followed.

Suddenly, Cody's face was smooched up against the glass. Things had gotten very tight ... and it wasn't the teleporter's fault.

"Willard?"

"Yeah, Cody?"

"Maybe you better cut down on those cookies and chips."

"Wouldn't hurt," Willard agreed. With some effort he was able to move his hand up to the keyboard. With greater effort he raised the hand holding Piper's email. "Okay, stand by."

"Willard?"

"Yeah, Cody?"

"If we die, you're going to live to regret it."

●

"Are you okay?" Zach whispered.

"Yeah," Ashley said. She was tied in a chair back-to-back with Zach. "I'm so sorry I got you into this."

He wasn't sure, but it sounded like she was crying again. "It's not your fault," he said. "You didn't know—"

"Silence!" Jason ordered.

"What are you going to do with us?" Zach demanded.

"It's not you I'm interested in."

Zach felt another cold chill. "Who...who else is there?"

Jason's lips curled into a menacing grin. "I think we both know. And if my spirit guide is correct, he should be here any—"

There was a knock on the door.

Jason's grin grew bigger.

More knocking. "Zach?" Piper's voice called. "Zach, you in there?"

Zach's heart sank as Jason signaled for Big Red to open the door.

●

"What's wrong?" Cody shouted from inside the phone booth. "Nothing's happening!"

"I'll need to boost the power!"

"What?!"

"We're bigger than hamsters and parakeets. Hang on." Willard punched more numbers into the keyboard. "There that should do it. Hang on!"

Cody waited.

He waited some more.

Nothing.

More of nothing.

"Say, Willard?"

"Yeah, yeah, I know, I know." Willard opened the door and stepped out.

Cody sighed. It felt good to breathe again. "What are you doing?" he called.

"I'm going to grab an extension cord and plug us into another outlet. Don't worry, it'll only take a minute."

"Take your time," Cody said. "Take all the time you want."

"Zach!" Piper spotted her brother and raced into the room.

"Piper, no! It's a trap! They want—"

The door slammed shut, and Piper spun around to see X-Ray and Big Red behind her. She reached out for Elijah's hand, but for some reason the little guy seemed unafraid. In fact, was it her imagination, or had he started to hum?

"Shut that kid up!"

Piper twirled around to see a skinny man with long black hair and tattoos. Immediately she knew it was Jason.

X-Ray and Big Red started for Elijah. She stepped between them, but Big Red threw her to the side like a rag doll.

"Leave her alone!" Zach shouted.

"Bring the boy to me," Jason ordered.

X-Ray bent down to Elijah. The boy looked up at him and hummed even louder.

"I said, shut that kid—"

Suddenly, the door flew open, slamming into Big Red's head, knocking him across the room.

And there, standing in the doorway, were Monica and her two goons.

"It's him!" Monica pointed at Elijah. "Grab the child!"

Bruno and Silas entered, and Bruno scooped Elijah under his arm.

"What are you doing?!" Jason shouted.

"We're, uh, grabbing the boy," Bruno explained.

"You can't do that!" Jason yelled.

Bruno looked at Elijah who was still smiling and humming. "We can't?"

"We're on the same side, you twit. We both work for Shadow Man."

Monica frowned and then reached for her cell phone.

"What are you doing?" Silas asked.

"I'm checking with the boss."

Suddenly, Jason let out a bloodcurdling scream.

Everyone froze.

"Oaff!" Jason doubled over like he'd been punched in the gut. He tried to stand, but the same invisible force hit him again, even harder. He dropped to his knees, coughing.

The group traded fearful looks as he struggled to rise.

He made it back to his feet and stumbled to the closest chair where he collapsed. By now he was gasping and choking like he couldn't breathe.

"Please ..." he cried. "Please, no, I—" It was as if he was fighting some unknown force. And then, suddenly, he went limp.

Everything grew quiet. Deathly quiet.

Then, ever so slowly, Jason raised his head. Though his eyes were shut, his mouth had twisted into a strange, creepy smile. He began to speak. But, of course, it wasn't his voice. "Well done, my friendsss."

Silas turned back to Monica. "You won't be needing to check with the boss."

"Why's that?" she asked.

"He's already here."

Chapter Twelve

Showdown

Piper stared at Jason as the voice continued to speak. "Make hassste! Bring the child to my compound."

Monica took a half step toward Elijah. "Yes, sir!" She threw a glance to Zach and Piper. "What about the brother and sister?"

"My ordersss are the sssame."

"Sir?"

"Dissspossse of them!"

Unsure what to do, Piper bowed her head and began to silently pray. *Dear God, help us. Please protect us from—*

"Ssstop her!" the voice hissed.

"Her?" Monica asked. "Her who?"

"HER!"

Piper opened her eyes and stiffened. Jason was glaring directly at her. Actually, more like *through* her. She'd never felt such hatred. For a moment it made her forget what she was doing … until she saw Zach. He had bowed his head and was also praying.

"Ssstop him!" the voice shouted.

Monica searched the room, trying to understand who Jason was talking about now.

But Piper knew. Encouraged by her brother, she bowed her head and continued praying—only this time, out loud. "Dear Lord. Protect us. Please help us to—"

"Ssstop!!"

Hearing Piper, Zach also began praying out loud. "Yes, Lord, help us. Jesus, we ask that—"

At the sound of Jesus' name, Jason's head flew back like he'd been hit. "AUGHHH!"

Both Piper and Zach looked up.

"Foolsss!" the voice shouted. "You dare challenge my power!?"

The table beside him started to shake. The brother and sister watched, speechless, as the table slowly lifted off the ground—an inch, then six inches, then an entire foot.

Piper's heart thumped in her chest. She was so frightened she forgot to pray.

Next, the glass ashtray lifted off the table. It hovered a moment, and then flew across the room, smashing into the wall directly behind her. Piper screamed. Come to think of it, one or two of the bad guys did too.

But the show wasn't over.

Jason began to laugh—softly at first, then louder and louder. As he did, doors around the house began opening and slamming. A mysterious wind came out of nowhere and, ever so slowly, Jason's chair lifted off the ground. His laugh turned into a mocking cackle as he raised his right hand and stretched it out towards Elijah.

Piper watched in horror as a swirling red glow appeared in Jason's palm. It grew brighter and brighter. Slowly it lifted off his hand and floated across the room toward Elijah. Piper wanted to scream, to yell at her brother to run. But she was so frightened no words would come.

The orb of light stopped just inches from Elijah's forehead. But, instead of fear, Elijah looked at it with fascination. It began to move around to the back of his head, then to the front again, circling him. Then again, faster. And again, even faster. And faster ... and faster.

But Elijah showed little concern. Instead, he started humming again. This time Piper recognized the song. It was an old-fashioned hymn.

"Ssstop ..."

A smile spread across Elijah's face. Slowly, he lifted his arms. He closed his eyes, tilted back his head, and to Piper's astonishment, the little guy began to sing.

"SSSTOP THAT!" the voice shouted.

Piper didn't understand the words to the hymn. They were foreign, like Latin or something. But she sure understood the impact they were having on Jason. He began squirming, tossing his head back and forth.

"SSSSTOP THAT SSSSINGING!!"

But Elijah didn't stop. Instead, he sang even louder. He was so happy that his face practically glowed. The red light that circled him faded, and then disappeared altogether.

"SSSSTOOOOPPP!"

Still grinning, still singing, Elijah finally turned to face Jason.

Instantly, Jason's chair crashed to the ground, shattering underneath him. The man cried out, but Elijah wasn't finished. He started walking toward him—still singing, still grinning.

"GET AWAY!" Jason scrambled to his knees. "GET AWAY FROM ME!"

Elijah stretched a hand toward him.

Jason scampered on his hands and knees to the far wall. "SSSSTOP HIM!"

But Elijah didn't stop

"SSSSTAY BACK!"

Elijah continued forward as Jason pressed against the wall, cowering. "SSSSTAY AWAY FROM ME!"

At last, the boy reached Jason. Elijah was still grinning, but singing softer now.

"SSSTAY BACK!"

Slowly, Elijah reached down to the man.

"SSSSTOP! DON'T TOUCH ME!"

But Elijah did touch him. And Jason screamed as though he'd been burned. "SSSSTOP IT! SSSSTOP IT! Ssssstooo ..." Jason collapsed onto the floor unconscious.

Elijah quit singing and looked down at the man with a sad sort of smile.

Everyone stared in absolute silence.

Well, almost everyone.

"Get him!" Monica shouted at her two goons.

But Silas and Bruno simply stared at her and blinked.

"I said get him!"

More blinking.

"Get him! Get him! Get—"

Elijah waved a hand in her direction, and she stopped shouting. It's hard to shout when you've fallen to the floor, unconscious.

"Hey!" Bruno cried in alarm. "What have you done to my Monica?" He started toward Elijah until the kid gave another wave and another body hit the floor.

Finally, he turned to Silas.

The man raised his hands. "Listen, I don't want no trouble." He started backing up. "Just let me go our way and—"

Elijah gave one last wave and one last goon hit the deck.

And Jason's guys? They were busy falling over each other while running out of the room as fast as their feet could carry them.

●

Mom and Dad scrambled up the ridge toward the Jeep.

The dogs sounded closer. A lot closer.

They arrived and flung open the doors, causing the car alarm to chime.

"The keys are still there!" Mom cried.

"Thank you, Lord," Dad said as he scooted behind the wheel. "Thank you."

●

Ashley, Piper, Zach, and Elijah raced down the porch steps and toward the diner.

"Hurry!" Zach yelled. "Before they wake up!"

"What went on back there?" Ashley shouted. "Does he do that often?"

Piper glanced to Elijah and shook her head. "Never. But with him it's always a surprise."

"Talk about power."

"It's not his," Zach explained. "As far as we can tell, it all comes from—"

"I know, I know," Ashley interrupted, "God, right?"

"He's got more power than a million of those

goofballs," Zach said. He looked at her and added, "And more love. Way more."

Piper threw a look to Ashley. She was nodding and thinking. Definitely thinking.

They reached the parking lot and the RV. Zach yanked open the door and was the first to enter when suddenly there was a blinding flash inside.

"What happened?" Piper shouted.

"It's your laptop!" Zach yelled.

"My laptop?"

"Well, not really your laptop. More like what came out of it."

"Hi, guys," a familiar voice said.

Piper stuck her head inside and couldn't believe her eyes. "Willard? Cody? What are you doing here?"

"You wouldn't believe us if we told you," Cody said. He was checking his arms and legs like he was glad they were all there.

"It doesn't matter!" Piper raced up the steps and threw her arms around him. "I'm just glad you're here!"

The only person more surprised than Cody was Piper. She immediately stepped back and cleared her throat. "What I mean is …" She glanced down, obviously embarrassed. "It's good to, uh, see you again." She stole a glance back up at Cody. The guy almost seemed to be glowing.

"Uh-oh," Willard said. He was glowing too. Not only glowing, but starting to short out. One minute he was there, then he'd blink out, then he was there again. "I guess … I … still don't … have … enough … power."

"What's going on?" Piper asked in alarm.

The blinking grew faster as Cody tried to explain " … another … Willard's … stupid … inventions."

"Oh, no," Piper groaned.

"Oh, yes," Willard shrugged.

And then, with another poof of light, they were suddenly gone.

"Nice of them to drop by," Zach smirked as he climbed behind the RV's steering wheel.

"Those were your ... friends?" Ashley asked.

"It's another long story," Zach said. "But we'll see them again, 'specially if Piper gets her way."

Piper glanced down, feeling her ears heat up.

"Get in." Zach motioned for Ashley to come inside.

"But, I—"

"We'll take you home."

She took a tentative step into the motor home. "But that's all the way back in L.A."

"Zach," Piper reminded him. "Mom and Dad are still in trouble. We gotta help them."

"She's right," Ashley said. "I can't put you out."

"Well, you sure can't stay here," Zach said. "Not with those creeps."

"I know, but—"

She was interrupted by the honking of a horn behind them. And more honking. And more. She poked her head outside and Piper joined her.

It was Gus the mechanic—sitting in his beat-up tow truck. "Will you kids move that bucket of bolts?!" he shouted from the window. "I gotta get this here fellow to Los Angeles and get back 'fore daybreak."

"Los Angeles?" Piper called, exchanging glances with Ashley. "That's a long way."

The old-timer jerked his thumb toward the passenger who was starting to climb into his truck. "He's paying me good money for it."

Piper looked over and was surprised to see the passenger was the gray-haired man Elijah had been studying the Bible with earlier.

The man smiled and explained. "Gus, here, says he won't have my car fixed for another two weeks, and I need to be in El Monte first thing tomorrow."

"El Monte?" Ashley asked in surprise.

He nodded. "I'm helping a youth pastor down there who works with families in crises—"

"*I* live in El Monte," Ashley said.

"Really?" the man exclaimed. "That's some coincidence."

Piper and Ashley exchanged a second pair of glances.

Ashley turned back to him. "Listen, you don't happen to have room for one more, do you?"

The man glanced into the truck and then called back. "Sure ... if you don't mind it being a little cramped."

"No," Ashley said, "I don't mind. I don't mind at all!"

As she spoke, Piper slowly turned to Elijah who sat in the motor home, humming away. Then she threw a look over to Zach who was obviously thinking what she was thinking.

●

Mom and Dad clamored into the Jeep. As Dad fired it up, Mom rummaged in the back.

"Here's the computer!" she exclaimed. "Can you believe it?! They even left our computer!"

"Great!" Dad pulled the Jeep onto the gravel road. "Send the kids an email. Make sure they're okay and tell them there's a little town called Bensonville on Highway 14. Let's meet up there."

"Terrific!" Mom said as she turned on the laptop and started to type.

●

Zach stood outside the motor home. It was harder saying good-bye to Ashley than he thought. "You'll keep in touch?" he asked.

She nodded, her eyes already filling with moisture.

"C'mon, boy," the mechanic shouted from the tow truck behind them. "Let's go!"

"He's right!" Piper called from inside the motor home. "We gotta hurry."

"Right." He turned back to Ashley. "I think things are going to work out."

Again Ashley nodded.

He cleared his throat. "Well, all right, then." Unsure what to do, he turned toward the RV.

"Zach?" Ashley's voice was clogged with emotion.

He turned back.

"Thanks."

"No problem." He felt his own throat tightening up.

"And what you said about God ... and all that stuff?"

"Yeah?"

"I'm going to give it some serious thought. I mean *real* serious."

"Cool," Zach smiled. Suddenly his own eyes started to burn.

"Zach!" Piper called.

"Well ... we'll see you then."

"Yeah," she croaked. "We'll see you."

Before he knew it, he reached down and kissed her on the forehead. Nothing mushy or romantic. Just a way of saying that he cared for her. Cared a lot.

She looked up and smiled as tears spilled down her cheeks. And then, without a word, she turned and dashed toward the waiting tow truck.

Once again the mechanic honked his horn.

"Come on, Zach!" Piper called. "They'll be here any minute. Move it!"

"All right, all right." He turned, gave his eyes a quick swipe, and stepped into the RV.

Piper sat in the passenger seat, working her laptop. "I got news from Mom and Dad."

"Where are they?" he asked as he climbed behind the wheel.

"They're safe. They got away."

"All right!"

"They want us to meet them in a town called Bensonville on Highway 14."

"Perfect." He reached down and turned on the ignition. "Bensonville, here we come!"

"What do you think about that, Elijah?" Piper turned to her little brother. "We're going to see Mom and Dad!"

Zach glanced into the mirror, expecting to see one happy little kid. Instead, Elijah sat in the back with a deep frown on his face. A very deep frown.

And that made Zach nervous—real nervous.

●

Mom and Dad continued down the deserted mountain road. Although exhausted from the ordeal, they were incredibly excited. In just a few hours they would be reunited with their children. And that thrilled them.

They might not have been quite so thrilled if they realized that underneath their Jeep was a small metal box with an antenna ... and a blinking red light.

●

Inside a black truck another red light blinked. On its roof a large antenna swept back and forth.

Two burly guards climbed inside. A third opened the rear door of the vehicle and waited as Shadow Man emerged from the building. Despite the lights around the compound, his face remained in darkness as he walked towards the truck.

"Are you sure this is necessary?" the guard asked as Shadow Man arrived. "We can find them and bring them to you."

"I mussst come along," Shadow Man hissed. "The boy isss too powerful to control from afar. I mussst be near to sssubdue and control him."

"Yes, sir."

He climbed into the rear of the truck, which had been specially outfitted to handle his large form. The guard shut the doors, and the vehicle slowly pulled away. As it passed through the gate, Shadow Man called to the driver. "Do you have a reading?"

"Yes sir. They're on the highway, 1.7 miles ahead."

"Good," the Shadow Man grinned. "Ssstay far behind them. We don't want them to know we're following until they meet up with their kidsss."

"Yes, sir," the driver answered.

"Then we will sssee who hasss the *real* power. Yesss, we will," he chuckled to himself. "Yesss, we will …"

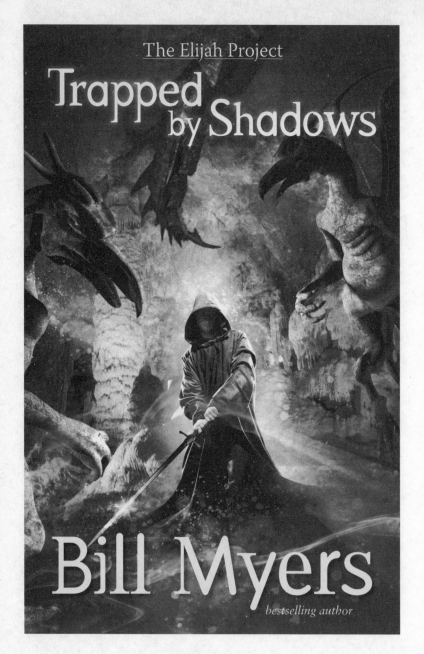

The Elijah Project

Trapped by Shadows

Bill Myers

bestselling author

The Adventure continues in

Trapped by Shadows

Chapter One

Pursuit

Thirteen minutes before midnight, three vehicles from three different directions sped toward a single destination, their occupants all focused on a single goal.

●

From the north, a mud-splattered Jeep Cherokee raced through the night. Dad concentrated harder as he tightened his grip on the wheel. His headlights caught a sign: Speed Limit 55. It whipped from sight as the Jeep slid around another curve.

"Mike!" his wife warned, her knuckles white as she clutched the dashboard.

"If we get pulled over, I'll explain our kids are in danger," said Dad, his mouth in a hard line as he stared ahead.

●

From the south, a sleek black Hummer roared down the highway. Its dashboard was lit up with indicators like the cockpit of a fighter jet: digital readouts, GPS map, radar screen, infrared monitor, and a flashing red light from the tracking device that had been attached to the underside of the mud-splattered Jeep, now only a few short miles away.

The glow from the dash lit the driver's face. He glanced into his rearview mirror, caring not so much what was on the road behind him so much as what was in the seat behind him — a dark presence that soaked up all the light around it.

Shadow Man.

●

And from the west, lumbering along as fast as it could, was an old beat-up RV camper. Its worn engine coughed and choked, puffing blue smoke out of its tailpipe.

Inside, sixteen-year-old Zach held the steering wheel with one hand while stuffing his mouth with the other — a Super Extreme Nuclear Burrito, featuring Flaming Fire Fajita Chicken. And forget the wimpy hot or extra hot sauce. Not for Zach. He'd gone for Taco Wonderland's newest sauce, the kind they advertised as *Danger: Explosive!*

Behind him, in the back of the RV, sat his thirteen-year-old sister, Piper. As the ultra-responsible one of the group (someone had to be), she was taking care of their six-year-old brother, Elijah.

"All right," she said, carefully tapping out some raisins into the little boy's hand, "you can have eight now and eight more when we get there."

Elijah, who hardly ever spoke, looked up at her with his big brown eyes and smiled—his way of saying thank you.

She smiled back. "Don't worry, it won't be long before we see Mom and Dad again. I promise."

Elijah nodded and laid his head on her arm. Piper tenderly stroked his hair, hoping she was right. Without her mom there, the job of caring for the little guy fell into her hands. Which was okay. She loved Elijah. He could be so sweet and caring ... when he wasn't being so weird. Honestly, she'd never met anybody like him. Sometimes it was like he knew what was going to happen before it happened. Sometimes when he visited sick people, they were suddenly well. And sometimes when the family really, absolutely needed something to happen, she'd see his little lips moving in prayer, and, just like that, it happened. Not all the time. But just enough to make things a little freaky.

And speaking of freaky, there was her older brother, Zach—it wasn't just his eating habits that were adventurous. It was everything he did. From seeing how fast a skateboard could go if you attached rocket motors to it (answer: ninety-three miles an hour before he crashed into a tree, flew through the air, and landed in someone's kiddie pool), to seeing how many bottles of ketchup you could drink before your hurl (answer: 1½), to talking his littler sister (as in Piper) into sticking her tongue on the frozen monkey bars in the middle of winter to see what would happen (answer: a visit by the paramedics who had to pour hot water on her tongue to unfreeze it from the bars).

Good ol' Zach. That's why she had to keep an eye on him all the time. Like now, when she looked up front and spotted him biting into his burrito. Like now, when his eyeballs bulged and his dark hair—which usually looked like it was styled by a fourteen-speed blender stuck on Super Chop—seemed to stand on end.

She could tell he wanted to say something. She could also tell that his mouth was on fire. Which explains why the only word that came out was:

"AAAAAAAAAAAAAH!"

"What's wrong?" Piper shouted. Then she saw the wrapper on the floor and understood. "Nuclear burrito?"

Zach nodded, waving air into his mouth, which caused the RV to swerve from side to side.

Piper sprang for the RV's sink. She turned the water on full blast and yanked up the sprayer, pulling the long hose to the driver's seat.

The RV bounced onto the road's shoulder as Zach slammed on the brakes, finally bringing the vehicle to a skidding stop.

"Open your mouth!" she yelled.

He obeyed.

She aimed for the screaming hole in Zach's face and pressed the sprayer.

The water hit its mark, and Zach's mouth sizzled like a frying pan dumped in cold water.

●

Meanwhile, in the Jeep, all Dad could think of was getting to his children before the other side did. He'd seen the evil their leader could do and he didn't like it. Not one bit. He wasn't sure if those dark powers came from this world or from somewhere else. Either way, the children had to be protected.

●

In the Hummer, the driver focused on the tracker beam and the GPS map. This time there would be no mistakes.

●

And in the RV, Zach's mouth continued to smolder.

Chapter Two

The Plot Sickens

There was a fourth vehicle: a dark green van sitting on the shoulder of the highway.

Inside, Monica Specter's red, shaggy hair shone in the mirror light. She was busy applying another layer of bright red lipstick and shimmering, electric-green eye shadow. Granted, sometimes in the bright sunlight all that makeup made her look a little bit like a clown. But in this dimmer light she looked more like a … well, all right, she still looked like a clown.

And don't even ask about her clothes. More often than not, it looked like somebody had just stitched a bunch of bright beach towels and bedspreads together and thrown them on her. It's not that she didn't have any fashion sense. It's just that … well, all right, she didn't have fashion sense either.

Bottom line: The same charm school that taught her all those delicate, lady-like manners (and she didn't have any) taught her the same delicate, lady-like ways of choosing her clothing and wearing her make up.

Bottom, bottom line: Monica was a real piece of work. Unfortunately, her partners weren't much better:

First, there was Bruno, a very large man with a very small brain.

Right on cue, she heard a cry of joy from the back-seat. Bruno had breathed on the glass beside him and fogged it up. He drew a smiley face with his finger ... to join an entire family of smiley faces he'd drawn across the window. "Wanna see me do it again?"

Then there was Silas, a pointy-nosed, pointy-chinned, pointy-everything guy with bloodshot eyes and big, droopy bags under them the size of hammocks.

"Not again ..." Silas sighed. "I don't ever want to see another smiley face in my life. Do you understand?"

Bruno paused in deep thought. "So ... you want me to draw little frowny faces, instead?"

Silas turned away and moaned.

"Will you two grow up?" Monica snarled from the front seat. (Snarling was one of her specialties.)

"I'm not the one who needs to grow up," Silas argued. "He is." He thrust a pointy thumb in the direction of his partner.

"No sir," Bruno said. "You are!"

"No, you are!"

"Liar, liar, pants on—"

"Knock it off!" Monica shouted. "You're acting like big, fat, stupid morons!"

Bruno sucked in his gut. "I'm not fat."

Monica could only stare. They had been sitting here

on the side of the road for hours, waiting for the kids' RV to rumble past. And they were definitely going stir-crazy.

But Monica was as determined as she was nasty. This time she would not fail. Shadow Man wanted the little boy. He never said why, but there was something very, very valuable about him. And she would deliver him. She had to. This was her chance to finally prove her worthiness.

She glanced at her two partners sulking in the backseat. They'd been assigned to her since the beginning—a skinny little weasel and a brainless baboon. They had bungled every assignment she'd been given.

But this time, it would be different.

Headlights suddenly appeared in the mirror.

"Duck!" she called back to them. "Duck!"

Bruno's face brightened. "You want me to draw a duck?"

"Duck! Duck!" she cried.

"Goose!" Bruno shouted back in glee.

"No, you moron," Silas scooted down in the seat. "She means *get down!*"

Silas yanked him down in the seat just as the RV swooshed by, rocking the van in its wake. Once it had passed, Monica rose and turned on the ignition. The van's engine roared to life. This time, the kid would be hers.

●

To anyone else, the run-down garage was packed with yesterday's junk. The sagging shelves bulged with old televisions, radios, and out-of-date computers. But to the inventor's eye, these old gadgets and circuit boards were the building blocks of imagination.

Willard, a pudgy genius with curly hair, punched in

numbers on his laptop. His reluctant assistant, Cody, watched with concern.

It was getting late, and they had to hurry.

"One more calculation ..." Willard punched a key on the laptop keyboard with the flair of a concert pianist hitting the last note of a great concerto, " ... and the program has now reached terminal status!"

Cody, who was definitely smart but not "Willard smart," turned to him and in his most intelligent voice asked, "Huh?"

"We're done!"

"Why didn't you just say 'we're done'?"

"I am a man of science," replied Willard, closing the laptop with a flourish.

"No, you're a guy who uses big words."

"Oh," Willard nodded knowingly. "You mean a *logophile*. Or a *logogogue*. Or possibly a *logomachist*. Or—"

"Willard?"

"Yes, Cody?"

"Be quiet."

Willard grinned as the laptop's lights flickered greenly. "I will gladly desist, my friend."

Cody started to answer, then stopped. Willard had always been smart. But lately he'd been testing his vocabulary ... and Cody's patience. A lot of people get their exercise by working out with weights. Willard worked out with words. Not that Cody blamed him. At school everyone made fun of him. Maybe this was his new way of fighting back.

Cody continued watching. "You still haven't told me how these are going to help Piper and her family."

"It will momentarily become clear," Willard said. "And you shall have nothing further to worry about."

Cody sighed, running his fingers through his hair. He'd heard that before. "That's what worries me."

"Here." Willard handed him two leg harnesses. "Put these on. They will assist in the stabilization process."

As Cody grabbed the leg harnesses, he thought back to some other not-so-successful-inventions Willard had recently created. Little things, like ...

The Solar-Powered Toaster that exploded into a fireball. Not bad, if you liked your toast well done.

The Computer-Guided Eyebrow Plucker. Unfortunately, it didn't stop with the eyebrows—as the first hundred angry, bald customers proved.

The Turbo-Charged Pickle Jar Lid Opener. A great success, except for the twenty-seven kosher dills still embedded in Cody's kitchen ceiling.

"Hurry!" Willard called over his shoulder. "We must dispatch ourselves with expedience!"

"Do what with who?" Cody asked, looking up at his friend.

"We gotta go!"

●

The map light illuminated Mom's finger as she traced the winding road on the atlas. "Just one more mile," she murmured. Her voice was both hopeful and anxious.

"All right, sweetheart," Dad said as they shot through the thick woods. He tried to sound reassuring, but inside his fear continued to grow. *What if we don't get to the kids before they do?*

He glanced to his wife and thought back to the beginning.

●

Mom had been pregnant with their third child, Elijah. She had just left the florist's with a giant bouquet of daisies for her sister's birthday. As she walked—more like waddled — toward the car, a bearded old man with a tattered jacket stepped in front of her, bringing her to an abrupt stop.

He spoke quietly, almost in reverence. "Your son will work miracles."

She blinked, more than a little surprised. How had he known she was going to have a boy?

He continued. "The Scriptures speak of him."

"Who?" she asked, hoping to slip inside the car and get away from the crazy man — not an easy feat when one is holding a bouquet of flowers.

"Your son."

She stared at him a moment, then nodded slowly, uneasily, as she opened the car door and got inside. She locked the car and put the key in the ignition. She glanced back at the man, but when she turned he had vanished. The old man was nowhere to be seen.

Unfortunately, that was only the beginning of the strangeness. It soon got stranger.

Just after Elijah was born, Mom and Dad began to notice little things. Like how their baby laughed and cooed as if he saw something above his crib ... when there was nothing there at all.

Or the time he was in preschool and his teacher ran out of snacks ... or thought she did. No one could explain how, when she kept reaching into the graham cracker box, she never ran out of graham crackers — not until the last child was served. Amazing. Well, to everyone but Mom and Dad.

That was the good weird. But there was also the bad ...

More and more, they got the sense that people were watching them. Sometimes it was a dark blue car that followed them at a distance when they pushed the baby stroller down the street. Other times it was a tall, skinny man in overalls who always seemed to be trimming hedges or sweeping a sidewalk when they went outside.

Then came the fateful Saturday morning when the strange old man appeared once again—but this time on their doorstep.

Spotting him through the window, Mom called upstairs to Dad. "Mike! That man from the florist—it's him! He's here!"

Dad bounded down the stairs and threw open the door to confront him. But the old man said only three words:

"You must leave."

"Guess again," Dad said. "I don't know who you are or what's going on, but you're the one who has to leave."

The man shook his head. "No. You must go. For the boy's safety—and your own."

Dad snorted in disgust and started to shut the door when the old man raised his voice. "Please ... there is an organization."

Dad hesitated.

The old man continued. "They are watching your son to see if he is the one of whom the Scriptures speak. Once they are sure, they will move in."

Dad frowned. "Organization?"

"They are empowered by a dark and sinister force, and they will show no mercy when they come for him."

Dad bristled. "That's enough. If you don't leave right now, I'm calling the police. Do you understand?"

The old man remained. "You've seen his gifts."

"I don't know what you're talking about."

"You've seen his powers. You've seen—"

Without a word Dad slammed the door.

"I'm not sure if you should have done that," Mom said.

"The guy's a loony!" Dad replied angrily. He turned, checking through the door's peephole.

Nobody was there.

That was when they decided to pack up the kids and move ... the first time.

But no matter how they tried to hide Elijah's special gifts, the little guy would do something that caused people to start talking ... and asking questions.

Then, just a few days ago, a red-headed woman and two men with guns showed up at the house. Mom and Dad tried to act as decoys to draw them away, giving their children a chance to escape to safety, but the plan backfired. Instead, the parents were kidnapped and taken to a mysterious compound where they first encountered ... Shadow Man.

They had escaped. It was a miracle from God — there was no doubt about that.

But Shadow Man wasn't about to give up — there was no doubt about that either.

Chapter Three

Arrest

"We're going to *fly?!*" Cody's voice cracked. It hadn't done that since he was thirteen, but raw fear can do that to a guy. "*AGAIN?*"

"No," Willard chuckled, "we're not going to fly."

"Whew, that's good."

"Technically, we will simply be resisting gravity."

Somehow, that didn't make Cody feel much better.

"We must locate Piper's parents," Willard said as he slipped into his antigravity tennis shoes. "We must inform them of the tracking device my equipment has discovered under their car. This is the only way to warn them."

"If we survive," Cody said, giving the shoes a doubtful look.

Willard ignored him. "I've triangulated their last email transmission with their cell phone call. But we must proceed there quickly before we lose them."

Cody was silent, frowning down at the tops of his tennis shoes.

"Look, I know what you're thinking," Willard said. "You're recalling the time my Remote-Controlled Pencil Sharpener flew out the window, crashed into the power station, and shorted out the entire town for a week."

"Actually," Cody said, "I forgot that one."

"Then perhaps it was my Inviso-Bug Spray which I brought to summer camp that made us both invisible."

"Actually," Cody corrected, "it just made our clothes invisible."

"Ah, yes." Willard nodded. "That was rather embarrassing. However, I promise you there will be no such occurrences on this occasion."

"Don't you think we should at least test them?" Cody asked.

"Under normal circumstances, yes, you would be correct. A positive outcome of a trial run is crucial before the operation of any new device."

"Good!"

"However, we have no time."

"Bad!"

"I assure you, all my data indicates these shoes will perform perfectly."

Cody gave him a look. He knew Willard wanted to help. He also knew that not a single invention of his had ever worked ... well, had ever worked the way he'd planned for it to work. Still, Willard was right. The family was in trouble, and they had no time to waste. So, with a heavy sigh (and a prayer that someone somewhere would someday find their bodies) Cody slipped into the shoes and laced them up tightly.

Willard reached for the control panel strapped to his wrist and hit a flashing red button. "Hopefully, we won't have any problems. Hold on."

"What do you mean, *hopefully*?" Cody's voice cracked again. "And what do you mean, *hold on*?"

"I mean...

"WHOOOAAAAAAAH!"

Suddenly Willard shot up and hovered in the air. For that matter, so did...

"WHOOOAAAAAAAH!"

... Cody.

There was only one minor problem.

"We're upside down!" Cody shouted, dangling from his feet. He kicked and spun around in the air as he tried to right himself.

"Yes, I am aware of that fact, however ..."

"However what?"

"We have no time for repairs! We must depart now!"

Before Cody could protest, Willard pushed a little joystick on his control panel, and they took off. Still upside down. And still shouting.

"WHOOOAAAAAAAH!!"

●

Mom and Dad pulled to a stop at the agreed-upon location: the parking lot of the Desert Sands Motor Lodge. They sat quietly in the Jeep, holding each other's hand, waiting eagerly and impatiently for their children. Dad tried to relax, nervously drumming his free fingers on the dash while Mom peered anxiously into the night.

"Mike!" she suddenly shouted.

He sat up and looked through the window, just in time to spot a pair of headlights coming up the highway. They belonged to the RV.

"It's them!"

●

Piper, peering out the window of the RV, gave a start. Her heart leapt as she cried out. "There they are!"

"I see them!" Zach exclaimed. He pressed down on the accelerator, urging the old vehicle forward.

Piper spun around and, in her excitement, gave Elijah a hug. The family would be together again at last. Maybe now things would finally get back to normal. No more kidnappings. No more escapes. Soon they'd be back home in the family room, munching popcorn, and watching the latest DVD.

The motor home pulled up beside the Jeep, and the doors to both vehicles flew open. Zach, Piper, and Elijah spilled out of the RV, while Mom and Dad raced out of the Jeep. Before they knew it, everyone was wrapped in one giant bear hug.

"Okay, okay," Zach gasped. "I can't breathe, give me some air."

Piper was enduring her own brand of suffocating, but the love felt too good to complain.

Finally they broke up, Mom wiping her eyes with the sleeve of her jacket. "Are you kids all okay?"

"We're fine," Piper said, blinking back her own tears. "What about you guys?"

"Couldn't be better," Mom laughed and threw her arms around them again for more hugs and suffocation.

"Whew," Dad waved his hand in front of his nose. "Son, what's that smell?"

Piper rolled her eyes. "Nuclear Burrito breath."

Elijah giggled as the family joked and hugged and teased. After all this time, they were together. How long they stood in the parking lot like that, nobody knows. But eventually, they split apart and headed back to the vehicles. Mom and the kids would ride in the Jeep, while Dad would follow behind in the RV.

It was time to go home.

●

Zach slid into the front seat beside Mom as she started up the Jeep and pulled onto the road. Elijah sat with Piper in the back. He snuggled against her and quickly fell asleep.

"I've got a ton of questions," Zach said.

"Me too," Piper added.

"Me three," Mom exclaimed.

"Okay," Zach said. "It was kinda weird when we came home from school and there's the vacuum cleaner in the middle of the floor—"

"Along with all the clothes from the dryer," Piper added, "and the dirty dishes piled up in the sink."

"Yeah," Zach said, "it was like you guys got raptured or something."

Mom nodded. "Okay, let me tell you what happened. I was watching the news on television when—" Her eyes caught something in the rearview mirror.

"What's wrong?" Zach asked.

Piper turned and saw Dad flashing his high beams at them. "Mom?"

"I see," Mom said. She had also seen the bright blue lights of a police car flashing behind Dad.

"Oh, no," she groaned.

"What?" Zach asked.

"Your father is getting pulled over."

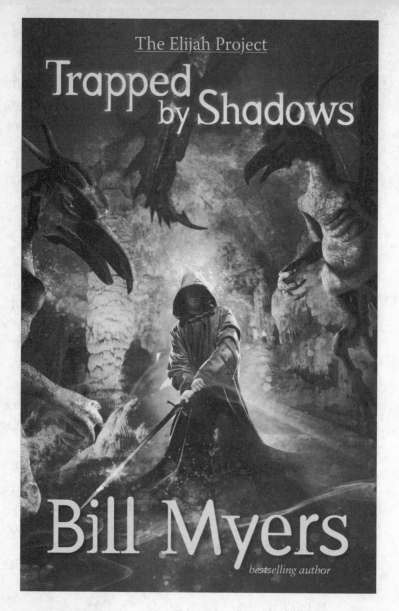

Trapped by Shadows
Softcover • ISBN 9780310711957

Elijah is captured, and his family must enter the Abyss to save him. The deeper they plunge into the caves, the greater the danger to them all, but they are not alone. Heaven is on their side.

Chamber of Lies

Softcover • ISBN 9780310711964

Zach, Piper, and Elijah are reunited with their parents. But when Elijah is lured into the Chamber, he must face the Shadow Man in a battle for his soul. Only heaven can help him now.

Available now at your local bookstore!

NIV Adventure Bible

Softcover • ISBN 9780310715436

In this revised edition of The NIV Adventure Bible, kids 9-12 will discover the treasure of God's Word. Filled with great adventures and exciting features, the NIV Adventure Bible opens a fresh new encounter with Scripture for kids, especially at a time when they are trying to develop their own ideas and opinions independent of their parents.

NIV Adventure Bible Book of Devotions

By Robin Schmitt
Softcover • ISBN 9780310714477

Get Ready for Adventure!
Grab your spyglass and compass and set sail for adventure! Like a map that leads to
great treasure, the *NIV Adventure Bible Book of Devotions* takes kids on a thrilling,
enriching quest. This yearlong devotional is filled with exciting fictional stories about
kids finding adventure in the real world. Boys and girls will learn more about God
and the Bible, and be inspired to live a life of faith—the greatest adventure of all.
Companion to the Adventure Bible, the #1 bestselling Bible for kids.

We want to hear from you. Please send your comments about this book to us in care of zreview@zondervan.com. Thank you.

ZONDERVAN.com/
AUTHORTRACKER
follow your favorite authors